THE WINO* NEXT DOOR

*WIFE IN NAME ONLY

VANESSA GRAY BARTAL

DRY CREEK PRESS

PROLOGUE

I wanted to be the first to tell the story because I know for a fact if she does it, I'm going to look like the bad guy. And I'm not. I'M NOT! I'll admit I married my quirky little neighbor for purely mercenary purposes, but she knew going into it what she was getting.

It was in no way my fault things went sideways. Did she say it was my fault? Because it wasn't. IT WASN'T!

I'm not getting upset, it's just...she does this to me. She makes me crazy. She looks cute and innocent, but you have no idea, none whatsoever, the insanity I've had to overcome in order to be here today.

The problem is that I don't know the best place to start. The beginning of our marriage? The first day we met? Her first day on earth? How far into history do I need to go to try and explain? It's like trying to look at the sky and pinpoint where the tornado began.

Give me a minute to get my thoughts together. In the meantime, do not listen to a word she says. NOT A WORD. It's like looking into Medusa's eyes, except instead of getting turned into stone, you'll become crazy. Trust me. I know.

*W*ait, he said that? He actually said those words? Would you care for some candy? Try this, it will change your life. Anyway, you can clearly understand the problem here was him. People that regimented are always secretly serial killers. No, I'm not saying I think he's actually killed someone. But there's a lot I don't know about him, I'll leave it that way. I mean, he doesn't have a basement, but the bodies have to be buried somewhere, am I right? If you take these cuffs off, I can arrange a proper plate for you. No? At least sip water between to cleanse your palate. Eat that one first, then that one. Like a party in your mouth. Now, where was I? Oh, yes.

I am not insane.

CHAPTER 1

She was insane. That was what he thought at his first glimpse of her. She must have been waiting and watching for him, proving his theory that she was a creepy stalker, because she poked her head out her door and spoke as soon as he arrived home.

"Got a minute?"

He hadn't been expecting her, hadn't been expecting anyone to accost him when he was about to reach his inner sanctum and unwind. So maybe he jumped and yelped a bit; it was only natural.

Did his neighbor have the good grace to apologize for scaring him? No, she giggled, a hand mashed over her mouth the only attempt to stifle her rude behavior. Before he could say a coherent word, for instance, "What are you doing here and were you waiting for me to get home?" she spoke again.

"Which appeals to you more?" He watched in amazed confusion as she reached inside her house and jammed her two fists in his face, each loaded with a bag of unknown substances.

"What?" he asked, confused and alarmed. Was she gifting him with something?

She sighed impatiently. "Which one, which one?" Her hasty, impatient tone matched the whole untethered vibe she had going right now—messy bun gone to the dark side of messiness, unwashed sweats that had seen better days, and was that…was that mango on the side of her face?

"I guess this one?" he said slowly, his words tilting uncertainly. He touched the one on his right, her left. She beamed at him.

"Me, too. Thanks."

And then she was gone. He stood blinking at her now closed door a few seconds before shaking his head—shaking off the odd interaction, really—and letting himself inside his apartment. *So that's my neighbor,* he thought, thoroughly unimpressed. He had sensed she was odd, based mostly on her nocturnal habits and continued invisibility. And this was his first glimpse of her: messy, bedraggled, and eccentric. He could only hope that would be his last sighting of her.

He set his briefcase beside the door, took off his shoes, set them on the tray, and loosened his tie. Then sat on the couch and let out the sigh that had been building since he left home that morning. *Home.* Dexter wasn't a sentimental man. No corny knickknacks lined his shelves, no picture of family or friends dominated his walls. But there was something so relieving about being home, about being free to be himself and not have to watch every word he uttered, every step he took. If people didn't believe the world of restaurant supply was cutthroat, they should try working for The Russians. Rumors swirled that they were in the mob. Dexter didn't believe them to be true. It was just that American culture was so different from Eastern European culture, so much more obsequious. Americans thought people were angry if they weren't overtly friendly, if they didn't smile for no reason. Dexter's half-Polish upbringing had taught him differently, had prepared him well to work for The Russians.

Who am I kidding? There is no preparation for them. The family was half intensely charismatic and half intensely psychotic. Dexter was the only outsider who worked for them, likely the only one who could handle their combined egos and rule branding. They partied hard and also liked to keep up the Orthodox pretense. *Enigmas, all of them.*

With as volatile as they were, Dexter was always in a state of insecurity over his job. He had the feeling they wanted it that way, wanted to keep him so off-kilter he was desperate to toe the line and hang on. And, really, they had nothing to fear from him. He was as solid as solid could be. And they paid him well, incredibly well, more than enough to cover the occasional emotional outburst that left him reeling or cleaning up one of their messes. And with The Russians, there were always messes.

After staring into the abyss a sufficient amount of time, Dexter wrenched himself off the couch and went to the kitchen to make supper. He wasn't one of those bachelors who ate out every single meal, but neither was he a secretly and dynamically gifted chef. He was mediocre, able to fry a burger or scramble an egg so he didn't starve. If he applied himself, he supposed he could get better, but what was the point? His boring attempts at creating sustenance had so far kept him alive.

The kitchen wall was the one that adjoined with his neighbor. They shared a house, one of those brick Victorian monstrosities that had been wisely broken down into smaller units. Their house only had two units, two halves of a too-big house. The neighborhood was a little shady and the price cheap, but Dexter was locked in, mostly because he told himself he was. He didn't like change, tended to find a path and stick on it forever. Some people might see it as a rut, but he liked ruts. Ruts were safe and secure.

On the other side of the wall, his neighbor dropped something big and heavy and emitted a word that sounded like something she made up to substitute for a curse. *Weird. So weird.* It satisfied him somehow that she turned out to be exactly as he suspected when he saw her things being moved in a couple of months ago. Based on the items he'd witnessed—a giant copper cauldron and a well-used boat oar—he thought maybe she was a witch. Some kind of latter-day earth mother who would steal snippets of his hair for her man-hating potions, then sell them to similarly embittered women. At least his sighting of her dispelled that notion. She hadn't looked like a granola cruncher or even embittered. She'd looked frazzled and exhausted.

His eyes fastened on the wall, in speculation this time. What could make someone so young look so panicked?

CHAPTER 2

Poverty. Or the threat thereof. That was what could put the fear into Lainey's eyes, what kept her up at night, working all hours. What drove her relentlessly to succeed, what made her purposely obtuse about how much she was failing.

Four months ago she was on her way to work when she had a near miss, a car going the wrong way down the interstate narrowly bypassed her and hit the car behind her. That car burst into flames, killing the woman trapped inside. The woman had been Lainey's age. They shared the same hair color, for goodness sake. It was as if death had been coming for her and decided at the last minute to choose someone else instead.

Lainey had stumbled into work that day like a zombie, paralyzed with the realization of how quickly her life could be over, and what had she done with it? *What am I even doing with my life?* She had stared around at her corporate job feeling the sort of panic one can only feel during the last year of the twenties. Then she went home and made candy. It was her go-to self-care therapeutic. She adored making candy, loved the way the ingredients came together like a science experiment. How could sugar and water come together to make a beautiful lollipop? Magic!

It was while she was making her nightly batch of candy, feeling soothed and happy for the first time all day, that she had the life-changing epiphany: *If making candy is what makes me happy, why don't I make candy?*

In that moment, it had felt so easy, so obvious. Of *course* she should quit her job and make candy fulltime. Why not?

Money, for one thing. She'd had to leave her semi-swanky apartment in the good part of town to move to a Victorian on the wrong side of the tracks. That in itself wouldn't have bothered her because she loved the old behemoths. But some monster had violently chopped the house into pieces, portioning off its beauty to tenants for a song. *At least this one was only cut in half,* she thought, pressing her hand to the brick wall of her kitchen. Unlike some of the others that had been butchered into quarters or even sixths like an unlucky brick chicken. Her bedroom had fifteen-foot ceilings; the kitchen had enough space for her supplies and then some. If she closed her eyes, she could pretend it was whole and unbroken, that the unseemly wall running through her kitchen didn't connect to what once belonged.

Lainey thought she understood stress, working as a corporate shill, but absolutely nothing compared to being her own boss. She was the one who had to do every drop of work in her new venture, and its success or failure also rested solely on her. She wasn't certain she had slept a full night since she quit her job.

On the other side of her wall, the tenant got out a pan and began frying something. Lainey grimaced, imagining the state of his arteries. Not that she was currently one to talk. She'd been subsisting on peanut butter and the occasional pretzel for the last few days. Not only because she was nearing the end of her limited funds, but also because she hadn't had time to do anything more than work. Certainly no time to make a proper meal or go to the grocery store. *Later, I'll get to it later,* she promised herself.

In the meantime, she had a satisfyingly full order of custom chocolates. All she had to do was finish and deliver the order and she'd have enough to last her until the next order came through. *What if the next order doesn't come through?* That mean little voice was so good at whispering those little doubts in her ear.

Shut up, it'll happen. Everything will be fine, you'll see.

Even though she shouted the words at herself, somehow the whisper was far easier to believe.

CHAPTER 3

The second time Dexter met Lainey was no less memorable.

"Sugar," she called as they were about to pass each other on the sidewalk, she coming home, he going out.

For a moment he was so befuddled he thought she was asking for a kiss. His lips almost puckered before realizing no person in her right mind would call out "sugar" on the sidewalk in demand of affection. The woman was bizarre, but not that bizarre, was she?

"Excuse me?" he said. He stopped short, which in itself was irritating. Dexter was a person who walked with purpose, always. Definitely not one to meander. He knew exactly how long it took to get to work, had it prescribed down to the nanosecond, and there could be no delay. Except now there was, in the form of his fellow house dweller.

"Sugar." She reached behind her to give the cart she was hauling a little pat. "Fifty pounds of it. Along with some lettuce, because I could feel scurvy settling in. It's not only a pirate disease. Something to keep in mind. And that's my neighborly advice to you for the day. You're welcome."

And then she kept walking, leaving Dexter to stare after her in openmouthed stupefaction. "You're not going to eat fifty pounds of sugar, are you?" he called.

"Obviously no," she returned without looking back.

He remained staring after her, mind now whirring. If she wasn't going to eat it, what did she intend to do with it? Sugar art? Was there such a thing? Bait rat traps? He shuddered, dearly hoping that wasn't what it was for.

When he realized how long he'd been standing in the middle of the sidewalk, mouth ajar, he snapped his jaw shut, faced forward, and marched with renewed purpose. He was going to be late. The Russians wouldn't like that.

"You are late. I don't like that," were his boss's greeting words. One of his bosses. Really, they were all his bosses. Sometimes Dexter thought the only reason they kept him around was to make themselves feel superior to each other by seeing who could order him around more.

"My neighbor," Dexter said, with a small shake of his head. They were certain to understand neighbor disputes because none of them could get along with their neighbors. He would say they couldn't get along with anyone outside the family, but no one within the family seemed to be able to get along, either.

Yuri, one of the brothers, made that Russian sound in the back of his throat that could either express disgust or affection. Dexter was fairly certain it wasn't affection, but he didn't know if the disgust was for him or on his behalf. He chose to believe the latter, which was exhibit four thousand in why he still got along with The Russians.

"Big meeting today. Big," Yuri said, his fingers rasping on his stubbled chin. All of the Russians could grow hair faster than kudzu, another way Dexter was different. His hair grew in an orderly fashion, like everything else on his body. Yuri let the last word hang expectantly. *Beeeg.* So dramatic, The Russians.

"We're ready," Dexter assured him.

Yuri quirked a dubious eyebrow at him. If he weren't at work and expected to be busy, he could sit and study them for hours. The things they could do with a flick of expression, better than any actor on a stage. "Yes? You sound sure for a man who was late today."

Dexter didn't remind him it was the first time he'd ever been late. In fact he didn't say a word, merely maintained eye contact that somehow worked as reassurance. Most of what Dexter did for The Russians was to put out fires, and most of those fires were of their own making. Some of those fires didn't even exist outside their minds. He was their American reassurance, a sort of cultural ambassador who bridged the gap between their abrupt and overheated passion and the unfathomable—at least to them—temperaments of the Americans who were their clients. They never said as much, of course, but Dexter was aware how much the company had grown under his watchful care. Before him they were seen as too volatile, almost toxic. After his calming presence, they became big players in the restaurant industry, now supplying some of the highest end establishments in the world.

"Should we bring in Sonya, eh?" Yuri asked, revealing his insecurity over the coming meeting.

Dexter's head snapped up. "No, absolutely not. Whatever you do, do not bring in Sonya." There were four Popov brothers, Yuri, Maxim, Ivan, and Andrei. Despite their bluster and machismo, Dexter could handle them fine. But their sister, Sonya, was another matter, a complete loose canon under no one's behest. Worse, she had a thing for Dexter, if one defined 'thing' as her predatory desire to use him and cast him away. The thing was, Sonya was a beautiful woman. From his perspective, the brothers were ugly—big, barrel chested, hairy, and brutish, women nonetheless seemed to find them attractive. But Sonya was like some leftover fairy from the Russian ballet. Delicate and shapely with porcelain skin, black hair, and deep blue eyes, she was the stuff of dreams. Or possibly nightmares. The Russians, being The Russians, believed Sonya was their secret weapon, that her beauty could overcome anything and get them entrée into all the places they wanted to be. But once again they failed to factor her extreme unpredictability into the equation. Sure, she could use her beauty to tame men. But she could also use it to punish them, to tease them, to anger them. And when she felt she wasn't getting her just due, she became pouty and resentful, eventually unhinged, and then all bets were off. No one wanted a knife around when Sonya was in a mood, that was for certain.

Dexter took a breath. "Look, Yuri, we have this, okay? The presentation is solid. Let's stick to the plan. And part of the plan is to let me have a few minutes to focus on that presentation. Go freshen up, make sure the lobby looks presentable, okay?"

"The lobby, yes," Yuri said, meandering away with a nod.

Before Dexter joined the company, the family did all business out of their warehouse on the docks, thus furthering the illusion they were in the mob. One of the first things Dexter did was to move them into an actual office and, not content with the cheap 70's décor, instituted a luxe remodel. Though The Russians had at first objected over the unnecessary expense, it was now their favorite place. On any given day they could be found in the marble and crystal lobby, more often than they could be found in their offices. Dexter thought maybe they saw it as tangible proof of how far they'd come. And, really, it was rather amazing that a family of immigrants now ran one of the premier restaurant supply businesses in the country, a multi-million dollar business spanning two coasts. If Dexter had anything to do with it, they would continue to grow and expand.

With that thought in mind, he opened his laptop and got to work double-checking his presentation. By the time the client meeting rolled around at one, he was ready.

They walked into the conference room in what was likely an intimidating herd. Though it wasn't his company, Dexter walked in front, the four brothers flanking him in a v-formation. Their secretary had already set everyone up with caviar and blini, another of Dexter's improvements. Their mother, bless her, liked to serve food to the guests. When Dexter first began, borscht had been on the menu. The smell of beets had been so strong it had been reason enough to move out of the warehouse and into the new office. Switching to the expensive caviar had gone along with the chic new face of the company. Their clients now were downing it like Skittles, but all munching stopped as everyone sat up and faced them.

Dexter tried to see his entourage from the new group's perspective. Four burly Russians and their Anglo herder, now taking all space in the doorway. "Good afternoon, Gentlemen," he said, his voice a soothing contrast to the glowering Russians. They didn't mean to look so cranky, Dexter knew. But whenever there was a client of this magnitude at stake, they became incredibly anxious. And because every emotion for them was first expressed as anger, it was always better if Dexter took the lead.

The necessary introductions were made and hands shaken all around. There were no women in the room and Dexter was disappointed. The Russians did better with a lady in the room. Perhaps because they were equal parts terrified and adoring of their little sister or perhaps because they were softies at heart. Whatever the reason, they tended to unbend easier with a woman around. With all men it would be hard for them to lower their combined guard. Currently they were scowling impressively, causing Dexter to have to be even more congenial. At least none of them was speaking. They told people Dexter did the talking because their English was subpar, but it wasn't true. Their English might be a bit broken, but it was stellar. The reason they remained quiet was because their manners were subpar, a lesson learned during Dexter's first month with the company when Andrei challenged a potential client to a wrestling match when the meeting started to go south. From then on, Dexter was in charge of speaking.

After the initial schmoozing was done, Dexter plunged in. With as antsy as The Russians were today, it was best to cut to the chase.

"I take it you've had a chance to peruse our catalog. You know what we provide, as well as our reputation for excellence."

His counterpart spokesperson, Bernard Geldof, leaned forward and rested his arms on the table. A piece of caviar dangled off one of his sleeves, looking like a suicidal fish egg about to take the plunge onto the table. Dexter forced his eyes not to stare at it in suspense, waiting for it to drop.

"Dexter, I'm going to be real with you all. I like a lot of what we've seen here today. Your products are excellent, your record for delivery, service and repair are incomparable. You are known for exceptional quality and that is exactly what we're looking for." Before Dexter could allow a small smile of triumph, he continued. "But there's something else your company is known for, a few whispers of volatile, unpredictable behavior. Now, I get that those might be in the past. In fact the rumors I heard were several years old. But our company, Bristol Brothers, is a hundred and fifty year old family company with a pristine reputation. We cater to an ultra-wealthy, ultra-discreet clientele. In this social media age where everything is recorded and wrongs are remembered forever, one whisper or hint of impropriety could ruin that reputation we've worked more than a century to build."

Beside him, The Russians shifted uneasily. Maxim slipped him a note. *Sonya?* Dexter crumpled it and slid it back. They were not bringing Sonya into this, not if he had breath in his body. He took a breath and pasted on his blandest smile, thankful for the average, everyman face he'd been given. It put people at ease, his lack of extremes. He was just sort of *there*, and it worked for him.

"Mr. Geldof, I understand. Believe me, I do. I will admit we had a few hiccups years ago when the company was young." *Meaning before I came on board and got things straightened out.* "But those years are behind us. I'm confident that no matter how hard you search, none of those rumors will have come from the last five years. And I'm also confident that no more will occur. The Popovs want nothing more than for their business to succeed. Their hard work on the company's behalf is what should be legendary because they are never not working." That part was true. The Popov family lived, ate, and breathed their company. It was so closely allied to their identity that he didn't think the family could survive if something happened to it. "We are professionals, solid and dependable, in every facet of life." He held eye contact with the man, oozing earnestness and honesty. For him those traits came easily. He had no idea what The Russians were doing at this moment. He hoped not glowering, as they tended to do when trying to look innocent.

Thankfully Mr. Geldof's gaze remained firmly fixed on him

instead of his bosses. "Can you assure me, with absolute certainty, that not one hint of scandal will eek from this company?"

"I'd stake my life on it," Dexter said.

After a few unblinking beats, Mr. Geldof jutted his hand and they shook.

The Russians kept it together admirably during the signing of the contracts and goodbyes. And then, when Geldof, et. al, were safely out of the parking lot, they let out a combined roar of happiness. Andrei ripped his shirt off while Maxim hopped onto the table and danced a little jig.

"Call Sonya and tell her to bring the vodka. Is time to party," Ivan called.

Dexter opened a bottle of aspirin and downed two, trying to ward off the coming migraine.

CHAPTER 4

"How's the roast?"

"It's great, thanks."

"Not too dry?" Lainey bit the inside of her cheek and waited for her dinner guest to answer.

"It's perfect, thank you. You're the only one outside the station who ever cooks for me, squirt." Ian tossed her a little wink, one that made her heart plummet, and resumed eating his meal.

If he had to give her a nickname, why did it have to be squirt? A forever reminder that she would be nothing to him but his best friend's unlovable little sister. "We have to take care of each other now, we who've been abandoned," she reasoned, hoping she sounded casual and not lovesick like she feared.

"True story, girl," he said, holding up his hand for a high five. "How is your loser brother, anyway?"

"You probably talk to him more than I do," she mumbled. Her brother wasn't the gooey affectionate sort, wasn't one for keeping in contact. She'd gotten much more warmth from Ian over the years than she ever had from Murphy, her own flesh and blood. Could that be why she loved him so? She grimaced. What she felt for Ian was not misplaced brotherly affection, that was for certain. It was something far worse—unrequited adoration.

"I ask you, Lainey girl, what does Florida have that we don't?" he demanded.

"Alligators, for one," she replied.

He shuddered. "Right. Gross. Are you going to taste them next time you go down?"

"I have no idea when I'll ever go down," Lainey replied. Her business was so new, her finances so tight, it would be too big a stretch to fly or even drive all the way to Florida. A spasm of fear gripped her chest but she pushed it away by focusing on Ian. He had been part of her life so long she couldn't remember not loving him, her older brother's best friend with a larger than life charisma. Even when Murphy had found her presence intolerable, Ian had welcomed her with a sweet affection, never impatient or rude. Was it any wonder she adored him? And then, after high school, he went on to complete his perfection by becoming a firefighter.

Lainey had never revealed her crush, obviously, but he had to know it was there. He wasn't blind or stupid. The thing she could never quite discern was if he played on it. And, if he did, did they ever have a chance at a future?

"What's up with you? I feel like we've been out of touch lately," she said. "I don't think I've seen you since Murphy moved." She'd made herself wait a reasonable amount of time before calling and inviting him for supper, not wanting to seem needy or over eager. But without her family in town, Ian was her only connection to her former life and she *had* been greedy. Greedy for a little care and kindness, for someone to take notice or an interest in her life.

"You know how it is, Lainey. Every day's the same and then you die," he said, tossing her a little self-deprecating smile that made her heart jolt.

"Not really," she said. Every single day for her was different since she quit her job. The only commonality was an unceasing striving for survival.

"I work, I sleep, I go out." He shrugged. "Adulthood, am I right?"

"Have you been lonely since Murphy went away?"

He laughed uncomfortably. "I don't know, Lainey. Guys don't exactly dwell on things like that."

"You totally should. Get in touch with all the gooey feelings inside you, Ian. It's healthy, I promise."

"Well, that's what I have you for. To keep me grounded." He tossed her the little wink again. She felt her cheeks heat and looked down to hide it.

"Guess what?" she said.

"I couldn't begin."

"I made you something special," she announced.

"Everything you make is special," he said.

"This is extra special," she declared. "Are you ready? Close your eyes. Are they closed? No peeking."

"I feel like we're ten again," he said.

"When I was ten, you were thirteen," she reminded him. She double checked to make sure his eyes were still closed, then set her surprise before him. He opened his eyes, blinked slowly twice, then burst into a puff of amused laughter.

"You made this? You made a chocolate fire engine? For me?"

"I've been working on my chocolate sculpture game. They're good for gift orders and I can charge a bundle for them." Mostly because a ton of hands-on work went into them, but that was neither here nor there.

Carefully, he held it aloft and inspected it. "Lainey, this is awesome. I mean seriously. But I don't want to eat it."

"It's supposed to be enjoyed," she said.

"I am going to enjoy it. And I'm going to take it to the firehouse so they can enjoy it, too. I'll tell them where I got it and maybe they'll order from you."

"Ian, that's so sweet. Thank you," Lainey said. She realized she was staring at him in abject adoration, hands clasped beneath her chin, and made herself look away. "Well, if you're not going to eat that, what do you want for dessert? Because I've kind of got a lot going on here, on the candy front." She opened a container and stared into it, jumping when Ian came close behind her to peer over her shoulder. His body pressed against the length of hers and she fought a shiver. It was far too long since she touched a boy, way too long since she had a date. Not that they ever ended well when everyone reminded her of Ian and came up short.

"That one," he said softly, his voice blowing warm on her ear.

Her heart began to thunder. *What is he doing? Is he making a move? Why now, of all times? Was it the chocolate fire truck?* If so, she'd sculpt a fleet of them. Before she could reach for the candy, he reached around her and picked it up, popping it in his mouth.

"I do love strawberry, Lainey," he whispered.

Be brave, she told herself and forced herself to turn around so she was chest to chest with him, face to face, minus her lesser height. "I know you love strawberries, Ian," she said, her voice a croaky whisper.

"You know all the things. Everything about me," he said. His eyes skimmed over her face. A heavy silence bloomed between them, thick with tension. They remained chest to chest, staring at each other, until Ian beamed and took a step back.

"This was the best, Lainey, thanks. I have to run, though. I've got a date. Wish me luck, squirt."

With that, he tossed her a wink, picked up his jacket, and jetted out the door.

CHAPTER 5

"How do you feel about pot roast?"

Those were his crazy neighbor's greeting words to Dexter when he arrived home that night.

"I have no strong feelings about it one way or another," he said. Her hair was back in the messy bun, but it looked tidier this time, straighter on top of her head and not slipped to the side like it was trying to escape the mess of her life.

She sighed, annoyed by his non-answer. "If a woman made you pot roast, how would you react? Would you think she was hitting on you?"

"I guess it depended on what she did with it. Like if she made it for me to eat, no. If she showed up at my house wearing only a pot roast, yes."

She burst into what was an arguably adorable fit of giggles and disappeared back inside her house.

Later, while he was still puzzling over the strange encounter, there was a knock at his door. When he answered, a tiny bundle of pot roast and all the trimmings sat in front of his door. He took it inside and inspected it, in case she'd shoved in any needles or other crazy person paraphernalia.

Crazy neighbor lady sure can cook, he thought, sitting down to eat the warmed over leftovers.

The next morning, Saturday, he laid the clean dishes outside her door and knocked. When no one answered, he turned and headed back toward his half of the house when, suddenly, her door opened but she was nowhere in sight.

"Psst," she whispered.

He froze and spun, facing her door and cocking his head. "Yes, disembodied voice, may I help you?"

"I said 'psst' and I stand by it." Her hand poked through the door and motioned him closer. Checking both ways, in case a bus came out of nowhere, maybe?, he eased tentatively forward. When he was as close to her door as he dared, her hand shot out, grabbed his shirt, and yanked him inside her apartment.

"Um, are you kidnapping me?" Dexter asked, wrenching free of her grasp.

"No, I'm saving you," she said. She looked rougher than usual, which was saying something. The messy bun had taken a dive completely off her head, dangling loosely by her left ear. She kept absently batting it away as if annoyed by the secrets it kept trying to whisper to her. Her eyes were hollow and dark-rimmed and on today's cheek seemed to be a streak of…strawberry? Yes, strawberry. The entire place reeked of it.

"What are you saving me from?" he asked.

"What?" she asked, blinking sleepily up at him.

He reached for a nearby box of tissues and used one to wipe her cheek, resisting the urge to tuck her hair more securely somewhere. "Why did you pull me in here?"

"The box people."

He stared at her, amusement morphing to genuine concern. "Are they with us here now?"

"What? No. They show up for deliveries and try to steal our packages. I have to keep a sharp eye out."

"I don't have any deliveries," he informed her.

"Yes, but if you did, I would keep an eye on them. As such, it's your job to help keep an eye on mine."

"Duly noted, though, you know, I'm not here most of the time." He took a step toward the door.

With a sigh, she pulled him back and, with another motion, herded him toward the couch. "I meant today. My tracking app says my package will be here any minute. I didn't want them to see you and get spooked."

"The delivery guy?"

"No, the box people."

"I thought you wanted them to be scared off," he said, thoroughly confused.

"Not like this," she said. "It's like you've never done package recon before. Rookie." She reached for a sucker from a tray to the right of the couch and handed it to him. He stared at it with absolutely no idea what he was supposed to do with it.

"What," he began but soon realized she was asleep. Worse, she had conked out against his shoulder, trapping him relentlessly in place. In his left hand he held a lollipop, in his right he held his weird little neighbor, and he wasn't certain which was more unexpected. He stared at her, willing her to wake up. When she didn't, he had the thought he should cover her with the afghan draped haphazardly over the arm of the couch. But if he moved, he might wake her or, worse, wake her in the act of covering her. There was something too disconcertingly intimate about being caught taking care of someone. So he remained frozen and watchful.

She was pretty, for a crazy person. Not insanely beautiful like Sonya, but it was Dexter's experience that the beautiful never seemed to be without the insanely portion. Unlike Sonya's glossy dark tresses, his neighbor's hair was multihued streaks of blond, thick stripes that looked as it had been painted by a brush. There were dark streaks and light streaks and what he thought was a gray hair that turned out to be glitter. Not for the first time he wondered about her. Why was she so exhausted? What did she do all night? Why didn't she go to work?

Maybe she was a telemarketer who worked midnights. That would explain her odd hours, as well as her oddly persistent personality.

Her nose had a little swoop on the end, like a Dr. Seuss character. Dexter resisted the urge to touch it because worse than being caught taking care of someone would definitely be touching someone's nose while they slept. But still, the urge was there, and that was surprising. Not that he was averse to women or wanting to touch one. But she was clearly on at least day three with that messy bun, rumpled, untidy almost beyond repair. Dexter didn't like things that were messy, especially not women. He put out fires for a living; he didn't want to have to do it in his private life.

The slamming of a door startled him out of his stare, focusing his attention back out the window in time to see the UPS driver arrive with the neighbor's package. And, almost as soon as he pulled away, a car drove slowly in front of their house and paused.

"The box people," Dexter hissed. Heart hammering with anxiety, he dodged off the couch and out the door to grab the package, bringing it inside with a triumphant slam of the door that did nothing to wake his sleeping neighbor.

In his absence she had curled into a tiny little ball on the couch, shivering like an abandoned kitten. This time he didn't hesitate before covering her with the afghan. Then he set her box on the floor, lollipop on top, and eased out the door and to his own side of the house.

CHAPTER 6

Despite their handful of interactions, Lainey hadn't actually given much thought to her neighbor. He seemed rather bland, an everyman. She was slightly amused by his overtly conservative buttoned down demeanor and she was thankful he was quiet and kept to himself. Otherwise, he wasn't much on her radar.

Maybe because lately the only thing on her radar was sugar and all the various ways to try and turn it into money, pretty, pretty money.

"Who lives in the other half of the house?" Ian asked as he sat at Lainey's table and watched her work. His head rested on his hand, face tilted and relaxed.

"Some guy. Seems nice."

"Nice, huh? Is that Lainey speak for a crush?"

"A crush? What am I, twelve?" she asked.

"To me, forever and ever," he said.

She frowned, realizing it was probably true. "Nah, he's not like that."

"Is he old?" Ian asked.

"No, he's about my age, maybe your age. And he's okay looking, kind of cute, actually. But he's...he's so *there*. I guess maybe I'm trying to say we lack passionate chemistry."

"Ugh," Ian grimaced. "Please don't ever say passionate chemistry again. It's like when your grandma says it."

"Thanks for that," Lainey replied, squinching her nose.

"You know what I mean. It's just…ew. You're so Lainey. Why are you doing that thing with your face?"

"Because the top of my nose itches insanely and my hands are covered in fifty pounds of chocolate," she said.

"Here, let me." He eased over and used a finger to lightly scratch the top of her nose. "Better?"

"Almost," she said, squinching again. He itched a few more times, angling closer to get a better hold on her.

"Now?" he asked. The contact had brought him in sharp relief with her body. Like last time, they were chest-to-chest, full contact.

"Yes, that's, um, that's good. Thank you."

He blinked down at her, smiling. "When did you turn into such a knockout, Lainey girl?"

"Um, never?" she said, resisting the urge to use one of her chocolate mitts to smooth her never-behaved hair. "I'm a chocolate-covered shame monster of no makeup and unwashed hair."

"You look pretty good to me," Ian said and Lainey's heart began to thrum. Was he hitting on her or did it only seem like it?

"Oh, that's, um, thanks? So, how did your date go?"

"What date?" he asked.

"The one you had the other night after you left here," she said.

He took a step back and resumed his seat at the table. "Oh, that. That was like three dates ago."

"Same girl?" she asked, hand tensing so the piece of chocolate she was shaping squished between her fingers. Impatiently, she shook them out and picked up another piece of chocolate.

"Occasionally," he said.

He sounded coy, but why? Did he want her to be jealous? Heartsick? Distraught? She was all those things and then some. It was the bane of her existence to believe he would one day find someone and get serious, maybe even marry that other someone. And then what would become of Lainey? No woman in her right mind would want her boyfriend/husband to visit his best friend's little sister, no matter how much of a mess Lainey might be.

The moment stretched. Did his glance fall to her lips, or was that more imagination on her part?

His phone beeped and they both jumped. "Whoops, gotta go," he said, taking a step back.

"Another girl?"

"Nah, another fire. Structure, all hands on deck. Check you later, squirt." With one of those winks that was becoming trademark, he was gone. And, as also was their custom, Lainey remained staring after him, longing and confused.

When she heard her neighbor arrive home a short while later, it seemed only natural to use him as a sounding board. Who else did she have, after all? She poked her head outside his door, trying not to startle him this time.

"What would it mean if you scratched a woman's nose?"

No such luck on the no-scaring front. "Bah!" he exclaimed and jumped about a foot as he whirled to face her. "What?" He pressed his hand to his heart. Lainey tried to tamp down her amusement, but it was hard. He was pretty fun to scare, especially because he didn't seem like the type to startle easily.

"Why would you scratch a woman's nose?"

"What? I didn't. Who said I did? Did someone say I did that? They're lying."

"Whoa, easy there, fella. Do you have some kind of secret nose fetish? I wasn't *accusing* you, I was asking you a generalized question."

"A generalized question about lady nose scratching?" he clarified.

"I said it," she replied, resolute.

"I don't know. Why can't she scratch her own nose?"

"Impaired chocolate fingers."

"Impaired chocolate fingers? Are you on crack?" He squinted, probably trying to see if her pupils were blown.

"Excuse me, but that type of psychosis would not be indicative of crack. It would far more explainably be PCP or Magic Mushrooms."

"Apparently you'd know, but why does it matter?"

"It matters to the psychiatric community that's been lobbying to make psychotropic drugs a treatment for PTSD."

"Are they the people with impaired chocolate fingers?" he asked.

"Obviously that was me," she said, exasperated. "You're not easy to talk to, do you know that?"

He put a hand to his head, as if in sudden pain. "Can I go now?"

"I guess so, but with the full knowledge you've been no help whatsoever. *Whatsoever.*" She jabbed an accusing finger at him.

"I'm going to back away slowly," he said and did exactly that until he was safely tucked inside his half the building.

Lainey went inside her own house and finished cleaning up the project she'd been working on. On the other side of the wall she heard her neighbor moving about, preparing his dinner. *Hamburger again.* It was oddly comforting to listen to his routine. Listening to his routine had become part of her routine, something she'd had much too little of in her life. Her family had moved too often to settle into any sort of acceptable patterns. Every time her father got what she and her brother called his "Pa Ingalls Look" they knew they would soon pack up and follow his latest venture wherever it might take them.

For a while they'd stayed in the same basic area, her mother's influence, no doubt. It had allowed them to finish high school in one place. Her brother, Murphy, had the rebellious sort of standoffishness that made him inexplicably popular. It was as if the harder he tried not to have anything to do with anyone, the more people followed him around, dying for his attention. Lainey, on the other hand, had been dying for someone, anyone to notice her and be friends. And though she didn't think she had ever been outwardly needy, it was as if people could sense the desperation on her and avoided her because of it.

While she was working, she'd had friends. But none of them had remained after she quit her job. And now she was isolated, with only Ian and her clean-cut neighbor for companionship, such as it was.

Her gaze strayed to their shared wall, wondering about him. Did he have family, friends, a girlfriend? If so, they never came to his house. No one came to his house. Was it possible he was as alone in the world as she was, and possibly as lonely?

Her heart lub-dubbed with a sympathetic little quiver and she purposed to reach out to him more, even though in her mind she'd already gone over and above. She had initiated several conversations with him, had left him a meal, and given him the last of her signature hand-made lollipops, one that sold for two dollars each at the farmer's market, thank you very much. Really, when she thought about it, the ball was now in his court for neighborly gestures.

Don't let me down, shared wall guy; I'm counting on you. She gave the wall a light pat, wondering if he could sense it, and returned to cleaning her mess.

CHAPTER 7

On the other side of the wall, Dexter did not sense Lainey's psychic directive. Nor did he feel any vibration in the force to tell him she'd patted their shared wall. In fact he wasn't thinking about her at all. His mind was solely on his hunger, his pending supper, his relief at having survived another week with The Russians.

They'd been unbearably cocky since winning the Bristol Brothers account, almost unhinged in their machismo and strutting. Whenever they were in this mood, they tended toward self-sabotage, meaning Dexter had to be especially on his guard. In the last week alone he'd stopped a parking lot brawl over, of all things, a gum wrapper, vetoed plans to send containers of spoiled borscht to their many enemies, stopped a plan to also begin smoking their own fish on site and sell it to their higher end clients, and successfully dodged three of Sonya's terrifying mating attempts. Before meeting her, he hadn't understood how men could be sexually harassed. He definitely got it now, he thought, shuddering as he tugged his sweater lower. Sonya was not a fan of the word no.

If he let himself, he could wonder why he remained in his current job. That was why it was always best not to wonder. It was what it was, and Dexter was a follow the groove type person. The Russians were his groove and he was stuck there, probably for life, or until one of them accidentally killed him by setting off fireworks in the office or some horror he hadn't yet thought to preemptively prohibit.

He finished his burger, cleaned up, checked his finances, and sat in front of the television to watch some sports highlights a few minutes before showering and slipping into bed. He had seemingly only closed his eyes when his phone rang, and since it could only be one thing that made his phone ring in the middle of the night, he was predictably less than enthused to answer.

"What?" he rasped, fumbling as he retrieved the phone from the charger where he placed it every night before bed, because routine was life.

"Why are you in bed?"

Dexter sat up, coming fully awake. He had expected one of The Russians, one of the brothers and even Sonya weren't outside the realm of possibility. But never in a million years did he expect a call from their mother.

"Mrs. Popov?"

"*Why are you in bed?*" she demanded, her rough accent making the words even more terrifying.

"Because it's midnight?" he said, a question.

"Do you know where my sons are?" she asked.

His heart started to thud. This was going to be bad, this was going to be very, very bad. "No. Do you?"

"They are at bar."

Dexter groaned.

"*Bristol Brothers* bar. To, and I quote despicable morons, celebrate giant victory with stuffy American corporation."

Dexter was already out of bed and throwing pants on. "I'll take care of it."

"Good, see that you do." She paused. "Should I send Sonya to help?"

"No," Dexter all but yelled, tossing his phone in his haste to pull a shirt over his head. Once fully dressed, he grabbed the phone and his keys and sprinted out the door.

Dexter wasn't one for speeding, but he did so now as he headed toward *Bristol Brothers* and what could only be certain doom. *What were they thinking?* They hadn't been, and that was the problem. Winning the Bristol contract had short circuited the tiny amount of self-control they possessed. Had they not listened when Bernard Geldof spoke? The one thing, *the one thing*, he asked of them was to remain scandal free. And now The Russians were bringing scandal to his home turf.

Any establishment owned by the Bristol family was the sort where there would be a line of Audis, Jaguars, and Teslas out front. Dexter screeched to a halt in front of the valet and tossed him the keys to his sensible, and therefore non-conforming, Honda. He sprinted inside, already hearing them before he approached. They were clapping, all four of them in unison, trying to get people to do the Cossak dance. Not that any of the four brothers could do it, but they liked to pretend they could by virtue of being Russian. (Sonya could, but that was another matter entirely, and one Dexter would rather not think about at the moment.)

The sight that greeted him wasn't as bad as it could have been, but it was still bad. The Russians rimmed the room, clapping loudly, while one very drunk old man was attempting to do the Cossak dance, squatting and kicking his legs out. Unfortunately he kept tipping over, giving everyone in the room anxiety about the state of his hips, to say nothing of his six thousand dollar Brooks Brothers suit.

The Russians caught sight of Dexter and froze, their claps stopping mid-air as they tried to shrink into themselves like startled puppies. He went to them one by one, rounding them up like an oversized nutcracker collection.

"Come on, Dexter," Andrei tried, cajoling. "We are celebrating, yes? No harm, look everyone is having fun." He pointed to the people who were still swaying halfheartedly, even though the clapping had stopped. Dexter might have bought it except one thing.

"Why is that waitress crying?" he demanded.

"Oh, well, they were out of the good vodka, and it's possible…" Yuri began, looking anywhere but at Dexter.

He sighed, not needing the rest filled in. They would have badgered and lectured her into tears. Hopefully a massive, immense tip would be enough to erase this, would keep her from complaining to her bosses. If they could just make it out the door with no more…

Too late. While his mind wandered, so did one of The Russians.

"Why does this place not have karaoke?" Maxim boomed, redrawing all attention on them again. "Who has microphone? I will sing." And, sans microphone, began to regale the room at large with the Soviet National Anthem as, one by one, the three remaining brothers began to join in.

Everyone was looking at them, more than their fellow drunk people at the bar, all the business people enjoying a quiet dinner in the restaurant began to poke their heads in. Waiters had to pivot around the gawkers, around The Russians. Dexter knew enough about the restaurant business to know what a massive distraction and disruption they now were. He had about ten seconds to end this and get them out before…

Too late again. One of the managers appeared on the floor. Worse, it was a member of the Bristol family. Why? Why did one of them have to be here and actually working on a night when The Russians decided to make an appearance? Dexter was usually quick on his feet, but as The Bristol approached him, his mind blanked. What on earth could he say to explain to their newest million-dollar client why his bosses were acting like a pack of drunk hyenas at the bar they were supposed to represent? The man came to rest in front of Dexter, bestowing such a look of disgust on him he felt the shame of it all the way to his toes. Without a doubt, they were done, not only with the Bristols, but probably anyone who had ever done business with them.

"Dexter."

"Mr. Bristol."

"I was under the impression that Bernard impressed upon you the need for absolute discretion and good behavior," Mr. Bristol said, voice stern and condescending.

Dexter, who hadn't done anything wrong, still felt the chastisement in every pore of his body. "You see…" he began, but Andrei interrupted him.

"Come on, Boss Man, is celebration." He threw his arms wide, slipping one around an unsuspecting woman who froze like a startled fawn.

Mr. Bristol, however, was properly distracted. "A celebration? What are you celebrating? Is someone getting married?"

Did…did he sound almost accepting of that proposition? If he thought they were there as customers to legitimately celebrate something other than the fact that he was now paying them to be obnoxious morons, could they get out of this debacle?

"Yes," Dexter blurted.

"You two?" Mr. Bristol asked, eyes squinting as they slid between Andrei and the woman who was now wriggling from beneath his heavy, hairy arm.

"No," she yelled, giving Andrei a shove that made him chuckle.

"No, it's um…" Dexter's eyes darted, frantic for an escape from the lie. He never lied, so of course he was predictably bad at it. Somehow he hadn't thought Mr. Bristol would ask any follow up questions.

And then, like a beacon, no, like a *miracle,* he saw his neighbor step to the bar, messy bun and all.

"It's me. I'm getting married. To her." He pointed to his neighbor. All eyes zoomed in on her while she remained completely unaware.

"What?" Yuri boomed. "I didn't know…" Dexter shot him a look that threatened to end him and he stopped speaking.

"Ah, well, Dexter, in that case congratulations. I guess that would explain a bit of celebrating," Mr. Bristol said, tipping his head at Dexter's neighbor. "Is she buying a jar of cherries from my bartender?"

"She can't get enough of them," Dexter said, nodding. "My girl loves her some cherries." That appeared to be an understatement as she received a giant glass jar of cherries from the bartender, tucking them under one arm like a precarious football. She turned to go and froze when she realized everyone was now staring at her. She looked wary until she caught sight of Dexter, then she smiled and waved and headed over.

"Hey, what are you...." she began but Dexter grabbed her and kissed her, cutting off her words.

It was a perfunctory kiss, but enough to stop her from saying anything incriminating, unless she responded by slapping him across the face which, given the circumstances, she totally could and he wouldn't judge her. But his eyes pled with her and she withdrew in silence, squint narrowed on him in speculation. Whatever brief interludes they'd shared had apparently been enough to buy him a bit of leeway.

"Hon, this is Mr. Bristol, the owner of this establishment and our new client I told you about," Dexter said, sliding his arm around her middle as they faced Mr. Bristol.

"How do you do, so pleased to meet you," she said, sounding like a non-crazy person for the first time in Dexter's brief experience with her.

"I'm good, thanks. And congratulations to you," Mr. Bristol said. Dexter gave her waist a small warning squeeze. "When is the big day?"

She glanced up at Dexter who was once again speechless with panic. Her brows rose infinitesimally. He tried to look pathetic and pleading, a thing which required exactly zero effort. "Soon?" she said, turning to face Mr. Bristol once more. "It was so nice to meet you, but I was in the middle of something, so..." she glanced longingly toward the door.

"Of course. I'll see you in a bit, babe," Dexter said, almost choking on the "babe."

She chortled, "Okay, *babe*," she replied and eased out of his embrace.

"What? That's it? That's so lame, is no way to say goodbye to future wife," Maxim boomed, starting to clap again.

I'm going to murder the moron, Dexter promised himself, but too late because the other brothers were also now clapping their encouragement.

"Real kiss," Ivan howled, and now all the other drunk people in the restaurant were clapping, too.

His neighbor must have realized there would be no easy escape. With a sigh, she turned to Yuri. "Dude, hold my cherries." Once her jar was safely deposited in Yuri's oversized paws, she faced Dexter and made a show of cracking her knuckles and neck. And then she stood on her toes, threaded her fingers in his hair, pulled him close, and gave him the kiss to end all kisses, one that had everyone in the restaurant cheering, especially The Russians.

And then, when it was over, she calmly reclaimed her cherries and walked out the door, with the eyes of every man trailing after her.

CHAPTER 8

It was two hours later by the time Dexter got all The Russians rounded up and deposited safely in their homes. He intended to slip back into a coma, but when he returned home his neighbor's light was still on. He knocked on her door.

"It's open," she called.

"It really shouldn't be. Not safe," he said as he opened the door and walked inside.

"Who else would it be but you?" he asked.

"I don't know, a murderer or rapist?" he tried.

"You're right, they're so polite and good about knocking," she said. She stood at her kitchen table, rolling something into balls, the giant jar of cherries open and half-used beside her. She noted what was in Dexter's hands. "Why are you carrying a giant jar of olives?"

"For you," he said, placing it on the table beside the cherries.

"Thank you. Is that, like, a custom with your people?" she asked.

"No, I thought they'd go with the cherries," he explained.

She grimaced. "Since when do olives and cherries pair well together?"

"No, not...You showed up at a bar to buy a giant jar of cherries. I thought maybe you had a raging cocktail addiction. It would kind of explain a lot, actually."

"Thank you, but no. I was making chocolate covered cherries and, due to poor planning, ran out of cherries. I went to three stores that were all inexplicably out of cherries before realizing a bar would have the size jar I needed. Voila."

"Why are you making chocolate covered cherries at two in the morning?" he asked, leaning against her counter as he watched her work.

"Can you think of a better time?" she asked.

"Yes, literally any of the daylight hours," he said.

"I don't really know if it's day or night anymore," she explained. "I've become one of the mole people."

"Is this what you do to fight insomnia? Make candy?"

"No, making candy is why I have insomnia," she said.

"Hmm," he said. Watching her roll each ball was oddly soothing and hypnotic. "So about tonight. Sorry you got sucked into my crazy work nightmare."

"Meh, it was fine. I figured it had an explanation I wasn't privy to," she said.

"You're being awfully laid back about learning I told people you're my fiancée," he said.

"I'm a laid back girl, Robert."

"Yeah…wait, who?"

"What?"

"No, who?"

"Are we doing a bit?" she said.

"No, you said Robert."

"Right."

"Who is Robert?" he asked.

"You are."

"No I'm not," he said. "My name is Dexter Niemen."

"Why did you change it from Robert?"

"I didn't. I have never been Robert."

"Are you sure? You really look like a Robert."

"I think I know my own name," he said.

"Yeesh, settle down. It's not like you know my name," she said.

"Your name is Lainey Andrews," he said.

"What? How do you know my name?" she demanded.

"How can you be outraged because I don't know your name and then appalled because I do?" he asked.

"How do you know my name, Robert?"

"Dexter," he amended.

"Where?" she said, turning to look behind her.

"I do not have the energy for your verbal shenanigans tonight," he said, swiping a weary hand on his face. "I saw your name on some mail."

"Ah, I should have remembered that tip from the stalker handbook," she said.

He rolled his eyes. "We share a proximity and I'm observant. Do you want some help with that?"

She froze. "Really? Why would you want to help me?"

"Why not? It looks fun, and it seems like you have a lot left to do."

"I do, actually. Some help would be nice. All you have to do is roll each cherry in a bit of fondant to make one inch balls." She held one up to demonstrate.

"Looks easy enough," he said. "Do you have a dedicated sink for washing hands?"

"Why would I have that?" she asked.

"Health department regul..." his words trailed off as he regarded the absolute chaos of her kitchen. "Never mind. I'll wash up at the sink."

"I'm not exactly a clean as you go type person. I wait until I'm finished, and then I clean. Also spoiler alert: I'm never finished."

"Right," he said, trying not to elbow a leaning stack of dishes as he washed his hands. He finished and held them aloft like a surgeon, searching for a clean towel.

"Paper towels," Lainey said, wrinkling her nose in the direction of the roll at the edge of the counter.

"Ah," he said, secretly relieved he wouldn't have to try and discern whether or not a cloth towel was clean or safe. He tore off a paper towel, dried his hands, and lobbed it toward the trash. It went wide. He sighed as he bent to retrieve it and tossed it into the can. Then he froze uncertainly.

"Did a trashcan kill your father?" Lainey asked.

Frowning, he spun to face her. "What?"

"You're staring pensively at my trash," she explained.

"I was wondering if I needed to wash my hands again, since I touched trash."

"Everything is trash eventually, Robert," Lainey replied.

"Dexter," he reminded her.

"Where?" she said, turning to peer behind her.

"Not this again," he muttered, moving forward to grab a glob of fondant from the bowl. It felt good, smooth, cool, and elastic. "This is like Play-Doh."

"Who told you my secret recipe?" she said, watching with approval as he retrieved a cherry from the jar, placed it inside the fondant gob, and rolled it into a smooth ball. "Hey, you're a natural."

"Not my first time," he said.

"Really?"

"Yes, of course it is. Do I seem like the type of person who rolls cherries for fun?"

"You could be anything. The world is your playground. And seeing you in your natural habitat tonight showed me there's a lot about you I don't know."

"Ditto, and that is not my natural habitat," he said with a grimace. "I go where The Russians go."

"How very Bolshevik of you," she said.

"How is your brain able to function like this in the middle of the night?" he demanded.

"It runs on a highly refined diet of sugar and maraschino dye," she replied. "Hey, you're really good at this." He deposited his fifth perfectly rolled cherry on the tray.

"Don't try to recruit me. The Russians pay too well."

"I can't actually offer you money, seeing as how I have none. But would you be willing to work for songs? Because I do an amazing Freddy Mercury impression."

"You hit on a lot of random men?" he guessed. When she puffed out a shocked laugh, it felt like a victory, in an odd way.

"No, but I do have a prominent overbite and mustache, if you look closely enough."

"Pretty sure I did that when you kissed me," he said.

"Oh, so we're going there. I thought we were going to pretend it never happened," she said.

"It definitely happened," he said. "And thank you for making it convincing."

"I'm an all or nothing gal," she said. "I never do a thing halfway. It's my passionate nature. That's also the explanation for my raging gambling, smoking, alcohol, and drug addictions. If I'm in, I'm going to be in until it kills me."

He thought she was kidding about most of those things, but who knew? Something was driving her to stay up night after night, to lose too many hours of sleep. He felt himself beginning to worry about her, and he didn't like that. The Russians took up too many of his worrying hours already. He could not add a crazy neighbor to the list.

They rolled cherries in fondant a while in surprisingly comfortable silence, until all the cherries had been covered.

"Now you sleep?" Dexter asked.

"Now I chocolate," Lainey replied, squinting. "I thought I knew how to make chocolate a verb. Turns out I don't. Thank you for your help with these." She motioned to the tray of cherries he'd assembled. In sharp contrast to her haphazard arrangement, his were in tidy rows, seven by twelve. She noted the disparity with a smile that might have been self-deprecating.

"Do you need help chocolating?"

"I can't ask you to do that," she said.

"You didn't. I'm volunteering. I'm vested now, might as well see it through," Dexter said. He sat, indicating that he was there for the long haul.

"All right," Lainey said, happily, he thought. She dumped a few massive hunks of chocolate into the copper cauldron and turned it on.

"'Double Double Toil and Trouble,'" he quoted.

"'Cool it with a baboon's blood, Then the charm is firm and good.'"

He stared at her, openmouthed and horrified.

"What?" she said. "That's the rest of the poem."

"What poem? That's just the thing you say when someone pulls out a cauldron."

"How many people in your life pull out cauldrons?" she mused, not facing him as she kept her focus on the chocolate. "It's from *Macbeth*. The witches' poem."

"Okay, professor," he said, embarrassed he hadn't known. Had he vaguely been trying to impress her by quoting something some part of him knew was high literature? Perhaps. But now that it had failed spectacularly he felt annoyed by the unintended shame he'd heaped on himself by his ignorance. Lainey seemed not to notice, however, as she continued to stir. "So this is what you do, you melt chocolate and bring down men with your superior knowledge of Shakespeare."

"Only on weekdays. On weekends I perform cabaret."

"With chocolate?" he guessed.

"Is there any other way?" she returned.

He watched, mesmerized, as she stirred and stirred the brown concoction that was rapidly becoming a liquid. When she was satisfied with the consistency, she pulled out a giant marble slab and poured the chocolate onto it, using some kind of implement to spread it out and scrape it together again, over and over.

"What are you doing?" he murmured sleepily. Watching her work was better than counting sheep. He felt like he was about to plummet face first onto the table full of cherries.

"Tempering the chocolate," Lainey said. After a while she scraped the chocolate back into the cauldron and returned to stirring, and then it was ready. He'd volunteered to help her dip the cherry balls, and he would, but for the moment he was caught up watching her hand swirl soothingly through the liquid. She held up a candy-covered hand.

"Impaired chocolate fingers," she announced.

"Are you trying to tell me your nose needs itched?" he asked.

"You'd like that, wouldn't you, nose freak," she murmured.

He snorted a laugh as he stood to move closer, reaching for his tray of cherry balls. "Yes, truly the one with a giant chocolate hand is the non-freak in this scenario. Spot on."

"You're about to acquire your own chocolate paw," she said, moving aside so he could dip with her. "Welcome to the club."

It was three in the morning. He should be sleeping and he didn't especially like being messy, especially when it was the sort of mess that oozed everywhere and got on everything. But as clubs went, it wasn't so bad.

They dipped in companionable silence until the sun rose. Lainey went to check on something and didn't return. When Dexter went to find her, he saw her asleep sitting up, one cheek mashed against the wall, drool running out the side of her askew lip.

He should go home and seek his own sleep. Instead he went to the kitchen and washed the towering stack of dishes.

CHAPTER 9

Dexter felt strangely upbeat when he went to work later that morning. Despite the fact that he was functioning on three hours of sleep and coffee, his mood was bright, his mind clear.

And then he arrived at work and found all the Popovs, minus Sonya, waiting for him in the conference room.

"Dexter, we need to talk," Mrs. Popov announced.

She was the second most terrifying Popov, with a lot of Sonya's authoritative instability, minus any of the sex appeal. She looked so much like a Babushka that Dexter always pictured her in loose baggy clothes and a head scarf, even though in reality she dressed fashionably, minus the fact that all her clothes were off-brand knockoffs. Currently her shirt was embroidered with little *Gucki* symbols, confusing Dexter for a moment. If one was trying to pass something off as authentic Gucci, why display the misspelled symbol for all to see? There were no easy questions with the Popovs, and similarly no easy answers.

Dexter waited to speak until he'd fixed himself another cup of coffee, his fourth. At this rate he'd be able to see through walls soon. He'd promised himself he wouldn't drink anymore today, jittery as he already was from the insomnia and rush of caffeine. But dealing with so many Popovs required an extra jolt.

"Yes," he said, sitting in the middle of the conference table across from Mrs. Popov. In fact he was across from all the Popovs. The parents sat in the middle of the large table, two boys on each side flanking them like a bird of prey. Despite that, Dexter wasn't nervous. Maybe he should be but something in him short circuited long ago when it came to dealing with The Russians.

"You owe us an explanation for last night," Mrs. Popov said, her accent thick and demanding, expression stern.

"I'm not certain what you mean," Dexter said.

She tossed her hands in frustration, causing all four of her sons to jump out of their sleepy stupors. "Last night. How did my sons wind up at that bar? You are supposed to be watching them. We *pay* you to watch them. Good money, Dexter. Don't pretend it's not." Here she jutted a finger toward his face.

"Mrs. Popov, you do pay me good money. I have no complaints about my salary. But I think our definitions of my job are different. I am your business manager. I procure clients and oversee day-to-day operations with those clients. Trying to keep your four grown sons in line is an extra pain on top of all my other responsibilities."

"I do not understand this insubordination," Mrs. Popov said, smacking her palm on the table, making her sons jump again. Seemingly the only women on Earth they feared were their mother and sister, both with good reason. "You know you are supposed to keep eye on them. If not you, who?"

Dexter made a slow survey of each brother, each at least two hundred pounds and over thirty years old. "Maybe they could look after themselves?" Dexter suggested.

Mrs. Popov snorted and waved her hand. "Impossible. They are, by far, too stupid. Let me be clear, this is why we pay you. To be the smart one. I do not want a repeat of last night *or else*. Are we clear?"

Dexter stared unblinking. It was an empty threat, he knew. No one else had the stomach to try and corral the Popovs. He sighed. "We're clear."

"Good," she said with a satisfied nod. She stood to go but Yuri spoke.

"Wait, wait, wait. We have to talk about the party."

His parents and Dexter turned in slow motion to survey him.

"What party?" Dexter asked, unable to mask his longsuffering tone.

"Yes, what party?" his mother echoed.

"The party for Dexter. For congratulations. He is getting married, Mama," Yuri said, beaming as everyone turned their attention to Dexter.

"No, I am not," Dexter said slowly.

"But you said…" Maxim added helpfully.

"Last night," Andrei continued where his brother left off.

"You told The Bristol you were getting married to Cherry Girl," Ivan finished, beaming.

Dexter stared at them, blinking, wondering how they'd survived this long, being this stupid. "I made that up."

Andrei's smile fell. "Made up? But why?"

Dexter surveyed their faces again to make certain they weren't joking. They were not, if their wounded, shocked expressions were any indication. "It was the only excuse I could think of on the spot, to explain to The Bristol why you were there disrupting his bar *after he explicitly forbid any hint of scandal.*"

"Oh," Yuri said, nodding. "Also *uh-oh.*"

There was a part of Dexter that didn't want to ask. He wanted to set down his coffee and return to a sane world, one that existed outside this office. In comparison even Lainey and her middle-of-the night chocolate making seemed normal. But, as Mrs. Popov so helpfully pointed out, that wasn't what he was paid for. So he took a bracing breath and made himself say, "What?"

Yuri cleared his throat, tossing his brothers a look that was clearly a plea for help. "You see," Andrei began. "We thought since you were marrying cherry girl, would be excellent time for party, yes?"

"And then…" Dexter prompted. Long experience told him they had only scraped the surface of the coming horror.

Andrei threw Maxim the conversational ball. "And then we invited everyone on client list to giant wedding party."

Mrs. Popov gasped, saving Dexter the trouble. She exclaimed something in Russian. Dexter had no idea what it was, but if the hangdog expression her sons assumed was any indication, it hadn't been a maternal endearment.

"But, Mama, is Dexter wedding, is celebration. Plus is party. Always good time for party, to show clients we are important and fun." Yuri held up his flexed bicep.

"Yes, fun," Andrei agreed, clapping. "I will do Cossack dance!"

The other brothers began clapping along. Dexter pressed his thumb to the middle of his forehead, trying to hold his brain in so it didn't explode.

"Fix it," Mrs. Popov said. When Dexter forced his eyes open, she was pointing at him.

"Let me recap, if I may. They showed up at The Bristol, creating a giant mess you dispatched me to clean up. While attempting to clean it up, I lied my face off, pretending to be engaged. And then they created a new mess by inviting everyone on the client list to a party for an event that doesn't exist. And now you want me to clean up that mess, too?"

"Is good recap," Mr. Popov said, nodding.

"See? He is smart one," Mrs. Popov agreed. To Dexter she added, "Yes. Fix it or you're fired."

"Maybe we call Sonya," Andrei suggested tentatively.

"No," Dexter practically yelled. By now his headache was a full-blown migraine. Between the sleepless night and the work nightmare, the last thing he needed was Sonya's terrifying form of flirting.

"Good, then we are done," Mrs. Popov said. She pushed back from the table, followed by her husband and each of her sons who were now conversing cheerfully with each other in Russian.

Dexter remained in the room staring at nothing, wondering how he was going to fix the current calamity, wondering where it all went wrong.

CHAPTER 10

"Guess what?"

Ian stood on Lainey's doorstep, looking fresh and handsome, unlike Lainey who woke with her face pressed onto the hardwood floor, rump in the air and hands mysteriously gripping the backs of her thighs. Had she been scooting across the floor like a worm? Who could say? And how much of the embarrassing position had her neighbor witnessed when he stayed to do her dishes? And now there was Ian, beautiful, perfect Ian.

"Someone offered you a modeling contract?" she guessed.

"Ha, not yet," he said, shoving his fingers into his hair in a way that increased his attractiveness by an impossible thirty percent. "Try again."

"There are hidden cameras out there filming a new episode of *Lainey Humiliation Time?*"

"I thought they canceled that after you sneezed out your retainer," Ian said, letting himself in uninvited before plopping onto her couch and putting his feet up. "You stink at this game, so I'll have to tell you. I have some orders for you."

"What makes you think I'll follow them?" she asked, hands on hips.

He snorted. "Lainey, you're so bizarre. Candy orders, insane person."

Her hands went slack, dangling uselessly against her thighs. "You got candy orders? For me?"

"Well, they're not for Willy Wonka," Ian said. "Some guys from work saw the fire truck and sent pictures to their wives who went nuts. They want stuff for kid birthdays, Easter, stuff like that. I wrote them down, along with their contact information." He tossed a little stack of papers on her coffee table and beamed up at her, awaiting the imminent fawning.

Lainey did not disappoint. "I love you," she blurted. In a hasty moment of horror she almost backpedaled, and then—fueled by lack of sleep and panic—decided to lean into it. "I mean I really love you. Like, in *that* way. I always have."

Ian blinked at her with wide eyes, his panic palpable. "Lainey…" he said slowly. She could feel the pending rejection, could almost see it hovering in the air between them, so she blustered on, powered by a need to dump all her humiliation on him at once and have done with.

"I want to marry you and have babies. Lots of babies. Your babies."

"Lainey…" he said again, and that was it. While she stood motionless and speechless, turned to stone by the magic of humiliation, he stared at her in horror, unable to find a graceful exit.

The moment stretched.

The silence hung.

Of all the embarrassing things that had happened to Lainey, and there had been a lot because she seemed predisposed to stumble into awkwardness, this was by far the worst. Because it was Ian, and she was stripped bare before him, the one person she loved most of anyone in the world. And now in a tangible way she realized she wasn't enough, would never be enough. She could see it, could *feel* it. He was top shelf; she was yesterday's leftovers.

Her eyes started to water, adding another layer of mortification, and there was nothing she could do to stop it. If she dabbed at them, it would only draw attention to the tears. But if she didn't do something soon, the tears would run over and create a river of shame on her hot cheeks.

"Lainey," Ian tried again, tone turning plaintive. He put out a hand as if to touch her, but he didn't connect. Instead the hand hung suspended, beseeching. *Please unsay what you said. Please rescue us both from this truth we'd both prefer to remain unacknowledged.* "It's not that I'm not…somewhat attracted to you. But I'm not…ready…for that kind of commitment. Not ready to take the plunge, and especially not with someone I've known forever. If things went bad, which they probably would, Murphy… Your dad… Long time…"

He seemed to be throwing out words and phrases now in the hope one of them would stick. Lainey knew she needed to provide a way out, a rescue for both of them. What she said instead was, "Please."

There's nothing men love more than desperation and begging, she thought as she watched Ian's expression shift from misery to revulsion. He took a breath and withdrew completely. "I just can't, squirt. Not like that. Not with you. I'm sorry." He looked helplessly around her apartment, probably wondering if he should force medicate her before he left, maybe a tranquilizer dart gun would drop magically from the ceiling, providing the stability she so desperately needed. No such luck, though. When it became clear nothing would arrive to end the awkwardness, Ian decided to end it himself. He dashed to his feet.

"I should go. Be sure to give them a call about the chocolate; it was a big hit." He forced a smile, as if to say, *I can't love you, but I did this good deed so you can never hate me.*

Lainey knew she should thank him for the chocolate orders he'd procured on her behalf, but she couldn't. She forced a tight smile and nodded, the tears now leaking down her face and plopping on her shirt.

Ian sighed, whether with remorse or frustration, she had no idea. Did it matter, though? The end result was the same. He didn't, *couldn't*, love her, and did she blame him? Would she love her, pathetic, needy mess she was? She was unlovable, had always been unlovable. This was only further proof of a deep truth she had always suspected but never verbalized. She was too much for Ian, too much for her father and brother, too much for everyone.

He let himself out and she remained staring rigidly into space, afraid to move because of the pending collapse. Finally she reached for the stack of orders he'd left on her table, a collection of names, numbers, and chocolate requests written in Ian's familiar and tidy block print.

Beneath those was another stack, one she had put off looking at. All of these had a red stamp across the top with some version of *Final Notice! Open Immediately!* Or something equally as ominous.

In addition to being a rejected, lonely loser, I'm about to be evicted and have my utilities shut off. What now?

There was only one thing she could think of that might work.

❦

*D*exter felt fairly defeated at the end of his long, terrible day. His headache had only gotten worse after the caffeine wore off. And after he learned his bosses were throwing him a wedding party for a wedding that didn't exist, the caffeine evaporated completely, leaving him groggy, foggy, and resenting every hour of lost sleep. All he wanted to do was crash, to sleep a few hours and try to clear his head. He did not want to deal with Lainey and any of her crazy, on top of the crazy he was already enmeshed in with The Russians.

But when he reached their front porch he heard a sound, a low keening sound that made him tip his head toward her apartment like a worried collie. What was that noise? Why did it make the hairs on the back of his neck stand up?

Ignore it, his pragmatic side told him.

Check it out, his cursed tender heart urged.

He waivered, hand on his doorknob a few beats until, with a sigh of annoyance, he went to Lainey's door and knocked.

The keening stopped but no one answered.

"Lainey?" he tried, hoping she would continue to ignore him. No such luck, though.

"It's open," her muffled voice called.

He pushed open the door, took a step inside, and stopped short. Lainey lay on the floor, arms and legs out in a starfish impression, face pressed to the wood as if they were making out.

"What are you doing?" He regretted asking the second the words left his lips, but he couldn't come up with any explanation for her actions, or for the woman herself. She was inexplicable.

"Grieving."

"Grieving what?"

"Everything. All the things."

He took a step closer. "What specifically?"

She rolled onto her back and squinted up at him. Her face was a mess of tears and grime. "It doesn't matter. Pick a topic and I'm sad about it."

Dexter plucked a few tissues from the box on her end table and sat down cross-legged beside her. "Is this something you do often?" He held out the tissues toward her. When she didn't take them, he leaned forward to wipe her face, pausing at her nose so she could blow like a toddler.

She shook her head. "This is something new. Five stars, would recommend this form of breakdown to all crazy people." She gave him a double thumbs up and resumed crying again.

"You're undoing my hard work of cleaning you up," Dexter noted.

"I'm a lost cause," Lainey wailed.

"Probably," Dexter agreed. He reached for another tissue, smiling when she laughed. "What's the problem, really?"

"Could you come down to my level?" She squinted and shaded her eyes with her hand. "It's hard to talk to you with the light behind you. Like trying to pour out your troubles to an angel."

He lay down beside her, stretching onto the uncomfortable floor with a yawn. "You know there's a rug right there. Easier on the hips."

"I needed the discomfort to match my inner turmoil. Self-flagellation for being the biggest idiot and loser in the world."

"You can still be an idiot and loser, but with padding. Doesn't make a difference," Dexter noted.

"I know," she said and, rolling toward him, pressed her face to his chest and began to cry in earnest.

Dexter, startled, did what came by instinct. He curled an arm around her and alternated patting and rubbing her back a few times.

"Oh, Robert," she wept.

"It's Dexter," he said.

"Where?" she returned, but halfheartedly. "This has been the worst day in the history of bad days."

"Hey, you don't own the market on bad days," he said, giving her a little cajoling shake.

She pulled back slightly to see his face, squinting. "Really? Why was your day bad?"

"My bosses…"

"The big Russian men?" she interjected.

"Yes. They thought I meant it last night when I told people we were engaged. They emailed the entire client list and invited them to our celebration reception. And now it's up to me to undo it."

She frowned at him a few beats and then burst into raucous laughter. "Oh, my goodness. That is the funniest thing I have ever heard. Did you tell me that to cheer me up? Thank you." She wiped her eyes again, but these were tears of laughter, he thought.

"No, I did not tell you that to cheer you up," he snapped, rolling away to put some distance between them. "You asked me why my day was a misery, and that's why. Because now I'm somehow tasked with uninviting a few hundred of the most powerful people in my industry to my fake wedding to *you*." He didn't have to add *and look at you, you're insane,* but it hung between them, an unacknowledged truth.

Lainey rolled onto her back and took a steadying breath. "Okay, I can see how that could be kind of stressful. Maybe you could find someone else and get married real quick. Any exes in your quiver you could make a go of things with?"

He stared at her in horror, convinced she was deranged. "You want me to call up one of my exes and *propose* to get out of work drama? Who does that?"

"You wouldn't have to trick them. You could be up front about it. 'Hey, I have this issue. It's tricky, but I think we could make it work. What do you say?'"

"If I were going to do that with any of them, I might as well do it with you," he said, squeezing the bridge of his nose in a failed attempt to ease the pressure. One of these days his head was really going to explode. Then they'd all be sorry.

"Ha," Lainey said. "I'm not that easy. I wouldn't do it for free. You'd have to sweeten the pot a little."

She was clearly joking, but Dexter's mind started to spin. By nature he was a problem solver. He had a problem, a big one, in his mind, and Lainey had just provided a possible solution. "Sweeten it how? With what?"

"Money," she said on a yawn. She closed her eyes, not realizing he was now studying her intently. "Lots of pretty, pretty money."

"How much money?" Dexter asked.

"Five thousand dollars," she said, clearly throwing out the first random number that came to mind.

"Okay," Dexter said.

She laughed, and then his tone registered. Slowly she opened her eyes and propped herself on one elbow, staring down at him. "Crazy pants says what? Also, are you hitting on me in some elaborate way that only people who iron and starch their clothes understands?"

He rolled his eyes. "Of course I am not hitting on you, yeesh. Give me a little credit."

"Oh, so you're proposing to me because..." she let the words trail.

"It's the easiest way to solve my current problem," he said reasonably.

"And create so many others," she said, gesticulating wildly. "We're talking about marriage here, an actual legal and binding contract. Not, like, you let me borrow a cup of sugar and I'll repay you plus two eggs. This is a grave life matter and you're bandying it about like it's nothing. Get therapy, you need it." She jabbed his shoulder and flounced onto her stomach, resuming the starfish position, along with the keening.

"Look, all I'm saying is think about it," he yelled. He had to yell to be heard over her forced grieving. "I have this problem, and you need money. We already live in the same house. All we have to do is get legally married, stay that way a while, and then quietly have it dissolved. Or even annulled. And I'll pay for that. There is no negative in this for you. You get the money you need and I get the wedding I need. We go to a big, Russian party, and that's that." He dusted his hands together to demonstrate.

Somewhere during his spiel Lainey stopped keening and opened her eyes, studying him. "I get that you're task-oriented and type-A, but this is a whole other level. This involves people and feelings and hearts. One or both of us could get very hurt."

"Why? We know going into it it's a business arrangement. We can even draw up a contract. It will be efficient and perfect."

"And someday when you're ready to get married for real, what will you tell the woman about me? 'My first wife? Just a business arrangement. You, though, you're the real deal, baby.'"

"First of all I would never call someone 'baby' unless I fathered her. Second, any woman I'm with will surely understand my pragmatic nature."

"Pragmatic nature. That's so hot." She fanned herself. "I do *not* have a pragmatic nature. What am I supposed to tell future Mr. Lainey? 'Some guy paid me to be his fake wife.' Do you know how that makes me look?" Her nose and lip wrinkled in sync. "There's a name for women who get money to do things like that, and I'm pretty sure it's not 'wife.'"

"Tell him it was a youthful indiscretion. Plus, not to point out the obvious here, but you don't even seem to be dating anyone. We might be discussing a hypothetical if you never get married."

The keening started again, louder this time, and Dexter began to think maybe this was all a terrible mistake, a sentiment that would only grow as time went on.

CHAPTER 11

"Think about it."

Those were Dexter's parting words to Lainey, after he covered her with an afghan and poked her on the shoulder through one of the holes. He let himself out, leaving her alone with her grief. And now she'd added another layer of humiliation.

Someone had asked her to be his wife, but in name only. As far as proposals went, it sort of stunk. And yet, try as she might, she couldn't seem to feel the insult in his words. Maybe because she was already maxed out on rejection. She wanted to call someone, to talk about the bombshell development, but who? Ian was the closest thing she had to a friend these days, and there was no way she was going to lay this train wreck at his feet. He would probably think she was making it up. *Sure, Lainey, a stranger* proposed *to you for the sake of his job.* She could almost feel the air quotes. But after her performance this morning, could she blame him for doubting her sanity? No she could not.

She reached for her phone and scrolled her contacts. She had a lot of acquaintances and former friends she'd drifted away from. Their precarious childhood, never in one place, made it difficult to establish lasting connections with anyone. Lainey had always found people to sit with at lunch, but that was usually as deep as the relationship went with anyone. She had hoped, rather desperately, that life would be different after school. She would find her tribe and have an active social life, filled with soul connections. The closest she came was occasionally being invited to go out with the after work crowd. None of them could help her now, nor would they want to. She couldn't imagine the reaction if she called one of her surface friends and dumped her current troubles in their lap. *I told my brother's best friend I want to have his babies and then the neighbor proposed.* Yikes, no thanks. They already thought she was crazy for quitting her job and starting a candy business. No need to add fuel to that fire.

That left only her brother. With a bracing breath, she pushed the button and called Murphy. And, as usual, got his voicemail. Knowing he was likely right beside his phone and simply trying to dodge her, she called four more times until he finally answered, annoyed. "Lainey, what?"

"Hi."

He sighed. "Hi. Why are you phone bombing me?"

"Phone bombing, is that a thing? Never heard of it."

"Lainey," he said, the intonation moving past annoyed big brother and into I'm about to hang up on you territory.

"I wanted to check in, see what was going on. It's this thing families do when they haven't talked in months," she said. Not that she'd know. No one in her family ever checked on her. Any contact was always one-sided, hers. "So what's new? How are you?"

"Nothing is new, everything is fine."

Chirp, chirp, chirp.

Lainey sighed. "Murphy, I just want to be involved in your life. I want to feel like we have a relationship. You're my only sibling. Doesn't that mean anything to you?"

"Lainey, why do you always have to make everything such a big deal? I swear it's like you suck up all the emotion in a twenty mile radius and save it to spew all over everything at inopportune times."

Lainey's eyes stung. As she reviewed her morning, she thought it was probably true. She was a ruiner; she ruined everything by feeling too much, *being* too much.

"All I want, all I have ever wanted was to be loved," she whispered, wiping her cheeks.

"And you are. Why can't you accept that it doesn't always happen on your terms? Just because we don't gush doesn't mean we don't care," Murphy said.

"If you never contact me, don't want to hear from me, couldn't care less what's going on with me, how exactly am I supposed to know you care?"

"Assume I do, unless I say otherwise," Murphy replied.

Lainey closed her eyes. Maybe he was right and she was expecting too much. Did that mean she had to accept painful silence and continued rejection as love? Who was right and who was wrong in this scenario? She had no idea. All she knew was that it hurt, and it took her back to her childhood, to being the unloved, ignored kid who couldn't count on anyone.

"Look, I gotta go," Murphy said.

"Okay," Lainey whispered, wiping her nose so she wouldn't sniff and annoy him further.

"I'll talk to you…soon."

"Okay," she said and hung up without her usual series of "I love yous." They were never returned. Usually she could laugh that off. Not today. Should she keen more? It hadn't actually helped, but she was no longer crying. What made her stop?

She rolled over and became tangled in the blanket Dexter threw over her. Her head tipped to the side, spying the tissue he'd used to wipe her face. She may not love him, but it was something, some connection in the world, some person who would find her body within a week if she tripped and died getting out of the bathtub.

Really, when she thought about it, it was probably the best offer she'd had in a while. Maybe ever.

Meanwhile Dexter went home and crashed. Sleep came hard and fast. After the energy he'd expended the last few hours, it was pure bliss to turn off his brain and go into a coma. He was lucky to be one of those people who could do that, could compartmentalize enough to shut off his thoughts and conk out. He pitied people with insomnia, he really did. It must be miserable to have to deal in the nighttime with what you tried to avoid during the day.

He woke at his normal time feeling refreshed, showered, and reached for the box of cereal when someone knocked at his door. Setting aside the cereal, he answered the door and found Lainey on the other side, looking subdued. She had also recently showered, allowing him to get a glimpse of her hair sans bun for the first time. It rested damp and curly on her shoulders. Her face was pale, eyes puffy and red. She did *not* look rested or refreshed. In fact she looked anything but. He was certain she'd come to reject his offer, so it came as something of a surprise when she spoke.

"I think we should do it. Let's get married."

He blinked at her. It had been his idea, but it was still a bit shocking to hear the words spoken out loud. "Do you want a bowl of cereal?"

Her eyes narrowed. "What kind?"

"Crack puffs. What does it matter? Are you really going to say no, based on what it is?"

"No, but I plan to judge you for your cereal choices," she said, closing the door as she followed him inside.

"Let's be fair: you're going to judge me no matter what," he said. He reached for the raisin bran, poured two bowls, retrieved two spoons, and motioned to the milk, indicating she should pour her own.

She did so and followed him to the table. They sat in companionable silence, chewing a few minutes, until he spoke again.

"What does raisin bran say about me?"

"Boring, steady, and predictable. All in all, not bad. I was afraid it would be something with marshmallows, then I'd have to run away and change my identity."

He laughed. "Why? What's wrong with marshmallows?"

"Nothing, if you're a marshmallow guy. If you pay more for your car than you did for your education, if you call everyone including your mom 'dude' or 'bro,' you can get away with eating marshmallows for breakfast and remain consistent. But if you're a guy like you—serious and responsible—who secretly eats marshmallows for breakfast, well..." She shook her head.

"What?" he asked, preemptively amused and exasperated.

"It would tell me you're hiding something, something bad. Because which one of you is the real guy? Mr. Responsible or Mr. Marshmallow? Way too uncertain to risk my future on."

"Why can't my name actually be Mr. Marshmallow? So cool," Dexter said. He finished his cereal and set aside his bowl. "So, what changed your mind? Yesterday you wanted to call the town elders and run me out of the village."

She scraped her bowl, staring at it, and gave a little shrug. "It seems like the best option to solve both our dilemmas."

He didn't disagree, but he wasn't comfortable with her tone. It was so...lifeless. Even in the short time he'd known her, he'd come to associate Lainey with passion. This colorless version left him feeling ill at ease.

"What's wrong, though? Seriously." He tapped her hand, drawing her eyes to him. They were swimming with tears. He handed her a napkin. She dabbed and took a shaky breath.

"There's this guy."

"Uh-oh," Dexter murmured.

She nodded her agreement. "I've known him forever and loved him as long. And yesterday I sort of...blurted. And he..."

"Didn't blurt back?" he guessed.

She shook her head and dabbed at her eyes again.

"What if we do this thing, get married for a few months, and a few weeks in he changes his mind and wants to be with you? Because I'm okay with not being in love, but I'm not great with my wife dating the love of her life," Dexter said.

"You should see a counselor for your possessiveness," she said and he smiled, relieved to hear a little of her old tone eek through. She took another breath. "I can promise you it's not going to be an issue. I know him and he doesn't feel the same. I knew before I blurted, but that's what I do. I blurt things. I spew my emotions on others like a fire hose, according to my brother."

Dexter gave her a sympathetic smile and handed her another napkin because she had soaked through and shredded the first one. "That's not so bad. Some people are blurters and some people aren't. It takes all kinds to make the world go round."

She gave him a watery smile. "Thank you, but this is me trying to be pragmatic. You have a job situation, and so do I. I need money, kind of desperately. As much as it makes me feel like a mercenary mail order bride, I have to admit that this is the best solution. But, listen to me being ever so rational, I think we should draw up an actual contract, so there's no misunderstanding."

"I think that sounds like a fine idea," Dexter agreed. He checked his watch. "But I also have to go to work right now. If I'm late again, I think The Russians might crack my ribs in some sort of punishment hug." He smiled when she snorted a laugh. "How about I'll pick up food tonight and we'll hash it out over supper. Do you have any allergies?"

"I'm apparently allergic to rejection," she said, giving her eyes a final swipe.

"Then I'll avoid the fried chicken place. They're pretty judgy and condescending," he said, smiling wider when she laughed again.

CHAPTER 12

Dexter could feel the tension in the air as soon as he arrived at work. He didn't understand it at first. The Russians never worried about problems; that was why they paid him. Despite the mess they'd made, they wouldn't normally be concerned over it, knowing he would somehow figure out how to solve it. And hopefully he had, if he and Lainey could come to some kind of arrangement. So it was odd and worrisome when none of them would make direct eye contact with him when he entered. And then he went to his office and realized why.

"Sonya." Her name always came out like he was in the middle of choking on a fishbone, a combination of her over-the-top beauty and terror. There was no way to be hyperbolic enough about her beauty, it was the Helen-of-Troy variety, the kind that launched ships, started wars, reduced men to rubble. It was so potent that Dexter always froze a few beats, acclimating himself. *So pretty. So, so pretty.* His hand would almost reach out, wanting to touch. And then sudden remembrance would come. He imagined it was the same with anything both beautiful and deadly. The beauty was always a lure for coming pain. Today was no exception.

Sonya smiled. Her perfect teeth were still hidden, but Dexter could picture them, pearly white and supernaturally sharp. He didn't know if that part was his imagination. He never let himself stare at her lush mouth long enough to learn if the teeth actually were sharper than others in her species, whatever that might be. Vampire? Perhaps. It was all too easy to picture her sucking the blood of some innocent dupe, himself included.

"So," she purred. She was that type of person who purred, who sashayed when she walked, who oozed sex-appeal and self-confidence. He got it now, why bombshell stars of the fifties had been such a thing. It was one thing seeing a picture of Marilyn Monroe and thinking she was pretty and another to see someone like her in action, an actual man-eater. "My brothers tell me you are getting married."

What exactly had they told her? That the marriage was a fake, for the sake of the company? Or merely that Dexter was engaged? Either way, the news wouldn't go down well. Since his first day at the company, Sonya had been trying to conquer him, to break him and leave him weak-kneed and devastated in her wake. There had been a few close calls when she almost succeeded, because her allure was that potent. Only Dexter's rigid self-control, combined with his solid work ethic, had kept her at bay.

"Yes." It was always best to say as little as possible. Somehow Sonya used every snippet of information to her advantage.

Her head tipped, eyes narrowing, but the smile remained. It turned frostier somehow, in that female way Dexter didn't understand. Women weren't great at saying what they meant, and Dexter despised games. It was one of the reasons he dated so rarely. "Congratulations."

"Thank you."

"When do I get to meet her?"

"Uh, wow, I don't know. Our schedule…" he glanced down at his watch, as if his calendar might be written there. In reality he needed a reprieve from Sonya's unfathomable blue eyes. It was like trying to stare at two sapphires. Eventually you had to look away for your own sanity because otherwise you'd be left wondering how anything could be so perfect.

"Surely you can find time for an old friend, yes? We go back so many years, Dexter, yes? I think I should meet this girl of yours, make certain she gets the Sonya seal of approval. After all, you chose her over me." There was no mistaking the way her words sharpened at the end.

"Sonya, you know that's not true. As I've told you, repeatedly, I work for your family. It's a conflict of interest for us to…"

She waved his words away with a dismissive hand. "Conflict of interest, bah. Everyone knows I run this ship. If I say I want to be with you, there is nothing they can do about it. Don't use my family or this company as an excuse. What it comes down to is this: you do not want to be with me. Say it."

"I have said it. Many times. You choose not to believe."

Her beautiful eyes filled with tears. Dexter wasn't moved much because she could turn the tears on and off like a faucet, according to her whims. But an angry or hurt Sonya was as dangerous as an angry or hurt wolverine. It would do to keep his distance and keep a wary eye. "Why don't you love me? Am I not beautiful enough for you? Is your love so much more perfect, more worthy?"

Dexter thought of Lainey, her half-falling apart bun, makeup-free visage, and chocolate-covered fingers and had to suppress a laugh. "No one is as beautiful as you, Sonya, which you know. It's not about beauty."

"Then what's it about?" she asked, stamping her foot.

Dexter wasn't certain he could explain it to her in a way she understood—that the predatory way she hunted him made him feel exactly that: like prey. But he had to try because the look in her eyes promised retribution, something he did not want to deal with, now or ever. "You are beautiful and wanted by everyone. I guess when I'm with a woman, I want to know I'm the only one, not one of a number."

"But you could be my only one. I have wanted you for *years*."

"But for how long?" he asked gently. Sonya wanted what she couldn't have. As soon as he gave in to her charms, she would win. She would break him and walk away, leaving him triumphantly in her dust. She didn't love him; she loved herself. She didn't want him; she wanted to destroy him for the sake of her vanity.

"I do not understand any of this. I do not understand why you push me away, time after time, why you will not love me. Maybe I am, as you say, a femme fatale, but I have feelings. And you don't care if you trample them."

Danger, danger, danger. Dexter began to feel muddled, and that was always bad. He didn't want to give in to Sonya's ploys, but what if it wasn't a ploy? What if Sonya genuinely cared for him and therefore felt genuinely rejected? He thought of Lainey, looking so pale and sad at breakfast that morning over some man's rejection. Did Sonya feel that way about him? He would feel terrible, if so.

"Sonya," he began in a softer tone than he usually used for her.

Seizing on the moment, Sonya stepped forward and kissed him, pressing him against the wall and running her hands over his flank like he was the hapless cheerleader and she was the over-eager high school quarterback.

After a stunned second he gave her shoulders a little shove. Being strong like her brothers, it did nothing to deter her. She only stepped back when she finished the kiss, with a triumphant little gleam in her eyes. "There. I bet it will not make your fiancée so happy to know you've been kissing your boss."

"Sonya," he said again, with renewed sternness this time. "Please go away."

Once again her face took on an irate gleam. "No one treats me this way, Dexter. No one. If I were your girl, I'd watch my back."

With that, she swished out of his office. He waited until she was fully gone before allowing himself to wipe his mouth and pop a mint. Sonya may look like a breath of fresh air, but she didn't taste like it. The times she accosted him with unwanted kisses always left him feeling a bit ill, a combined sour and bitter taste in his mouth that made him queasy.

When he finally sat and turned on his computer, one of those unsolicited pop-up ads jumped to the forefront, requesting questions for an online advice column. For a moment he let himself imagine he would send one in.

Dear Edith Jones, my boss is sexually harassing me. Please help!

But as always he pushed the thought away. Anyone with eyes would take one look at Sonya, one look at him, and call him the world's biggest liar.

⚷

*A*fter her breakfast with Dexter, Lainey felt numb. It wasn't like her to not feel anything, but she reasoned that she had expended all of her emotions and then some the day before. Just because she'd agreed to marry a stranger was no reason her feelings might have put themselves on autopilot. Because as much as she knew she should be appalled by the decision she'd made, she wasn't. Whatever he was, Dexter was a good guy. She knew it, she could *feel* it all the way to her bones. And in the end, despite the fact that she was lonely and needed money, it was that certainty that caused her to say yes. Dexter was in a pickle, and she had the means to provide a rescue. For once. There was something uplifting about that. Her life might be a moving dumpster fire, but she was offering someone else a hand up, a way out.

Maybe someday I'll get it together enough to always be that person, she thought. She hoped so. It was more cheerful to believe she might someday get herself together than to always believe she would be the total loser she currently was.

In order to further the myth that she was a functioning adult, she made her candy deliveries, went to the bank, and used the last of her savings to pay some of the bills she'd fallen behind on. And then she cleaned her house. It wasn't that she was a slob, rather she became easily overwhelmed by life. And when she was overwhelmed, she put the things that took the most energy at the bottom of her list. Cleaning and paying bills took the sort of mental energy she'd lacked since she became her own boss. Her mind was too occupied with trying to stay alive to worry about how long it had been since she scrubbed the toilet.

But on this day, the day after she once again took a wrecking ball to her life, she decided cleaning would help not hinder. And it did.

After everything was put back in its place and scrubbed, she felt more settled, less scattered, a little bit more in control of the chaos.

When Dexter arrived with supper, it was the first thing he noticed, naturally.

"Hey, you have a table," he said, setting the bag of good-smelling food on top of it.

"Ha, ha, Lainey's life is a catastrophe. Let's all laugh at the freak," she said, doing a slow clap for his lame humor.

"Okay, but first let's eat. I'm starving." He began opening bags and setting things out. "I asked for plates and cutlery because I didn't know it was cleaning day and I thought maybe I'd have to fight a rat for a fork here."

"For your information, I have never had ra… Oh, wait. I forgot about college. But in my defense, it was a really cheap apartment and I'm pretty sure they predated me, if the way they eyeballed me like I was invading their territory was any indication. I think I moved out in the nick of time before they started challenging me to duels with tiny swords."

"I would pay money to see that," Dexter said.

"I'll remember that, if funds get tight again," she said and he had to press a napkin to his lips to avoid spewing his food at her when he laughed.

"That's going to be first on the list," Lainey told him, finger jutted. "I need me a husband with impeccable table manners, like an Edwardian gentleman. You'd better know how to wield your oyster fork and on which side of you the duchess should sit. Also I require entertaining and thought provoking mealtime conversation."

"There's a company that turns dead bodies into ocean reefs," Dexter returned.

"That'll do nicely," Lainey said, nodding her approval. "Better save it for the duchess, though."

"Hmm," Dexter agreed, not pausing from his meal again until the edge was gone from his hunger. And then he said, "What is on your contractual requirements, really?"

"I jotted some ideas between cleaning tasks today," Lainey said.

She withdrew a giant tome from her bookshelf and sat it on the table between them. "Chapter one, Section A, line one."

"I think my first one is going to be 'no stupid humor,'" Dexter said.

"I'll be a mute," she argued.

"Then it's definitely going on the list," he said, mimicking zipping his lips.

She opened the book and pulled out her actual list. "You are no fun."

"That was coincidentally my nickname all through school," Dexter said. But he was curious about her list. Exactly how demanding was she? It was probably something he should find out before he tied himself to her legally.

"No sex," she announced with no preamble and he choked on air.

"Oh, geez, warn a guy, would you?" He sipped water a few beats while she held her list aloft, waiting him out.

"How would I warn you? Hey, guy, I'm about to say 'no sex.' Prepare yourself for abstinence."

"I don't know. I thought you were going to start with something smaller, like nuclear war or something." He took another sip and set his empty glass down with a clatter. "Never start with sex, Lainey. Too much, too soon. Pick something else and we'll come back to it."

Her eyes widened. "Because you plan to negotiate?"

"No, because I'd like to get through the conversation with my brain intact and now it exploded out my ears." He pressed his palms over his ears. "Pick something else."

"Fine. No smoking."

"I don't smoke."

"But I take it so seriously I'm adding smoked meats in there. Eat a smoked salmon, and it's over," she warned.

"Is there anything that's not nonsensical on your list?" he asked.

She glanced down. "Affection."

"Excuse me?"

"I demand affection."

"You *demand* affection? How does one *demand* affection?"

"I require one affectionate gesture per day," she said.

He stared at her, squinting a little. "Doesn't that seem wrong to you? Shouldn't someone give affection freely? Don't you feel bad about taking it by force?"

"Would you give it if I didn't demand it?" she asked.

He snorted. "No."

"Well, there you go."

"But it's so…debasing," he said.

She waved her hand up and down, encompassing her body. "Look at me. I'm on my last leg here. Literally the last thing left that hasn't been torn down irreparably is the freckles on the tops of my toes. And you think asking for a hug is going to humiliate me? I told a man I want to have his babies. I am starved for human touch and I have nothing left. If the least I can get out of this is a few pity hugs, I'll take them."

"You have freckles on your toes?" he said.

"You'll never know because of rule number one on my list."

"You have to be at that level of intimacy with a man to let him see your toe freckles?"

"I'm extremely protective of my foot freckles. Moving on, what's on your list?" she asked.

"It's hard to say because the list revised itself in my head so many times while you were talking," he said.

She made a "hurry up" gesture with her hand.

"You're not going to like it," he warned.

"I'm peering up at you from rock bottom, and you seem far away. Carry on," she urged.

"Okay. First off I wanted to be clear about what this isn't. We aren't dating. I'm not your boyfriend. This is a business arrangement."

"Emotionally unavailable and terrified of commitment. Got it. Anything else?"

He took a breath. "This is the part that's going to sting. I put out fires for a living, sometimes literally. I don't want to do that in my personal life."

"What are you saying?" she asked.

"I am not a fixer, and certainly not *your* fixer. I might occasionally drop by to roll some more cherries into balls or do your dishes, but I won't be that guy who swoops in and manages things and rescues you."

She barked a harsh laugh. "Let me set your mind at ease: I gave up on being rescued a long time ago. Yes, my life is a calamity much of the time, but it's my calamity, and I manage. Anything else?"

"Not that I can think of," he said. He jutted his hand over the table. She stared at it.

"What's that for?"

"To shake on it."

"Shake on it? What is this, the Treaty of Versailles? You don't shake on something like this."

"What do you think we're supposed to do?" he asked with more than a bit of apprehension.

"Hug, obviously. Affection, remember?"

"We're not married yet," he argued.

She rolled her eyes. "I'm about to jump off the marital cliff for you. I'm going to need preemptive affection."

"Just like that?"

"Just like that. Stand up." She stood, waiting impatiently while he rose as slowly as possible. "Put your arms out." He did so, curling them around her slightly when she walked into them.

"I don't know what I'm doing," he said. "This feels unnatural and uncomfortable."

"That's because it's the first time. After awhile you'll form a Lainey addiction. You need to loosen up. Nestle a little."

"Nestle? You make me sound like a bird arranging plumage in its home."

"Yes, that's what you should be. A boy bird trying to attract a female with his soft and cozy plumage pad." She poked him. "Nestle."

He twisted his head a little, burrowing. She barked another laugh and collapsed her neck, bonking him hard on the temple.

"Yow," he exclaimed, letting her go to press his hand against his throbbing head.

"Sorry," she said, rubbing her own head while still laughing. "I forgot to warn you I'm ticklish. That was pretty good for a first time."

"Should I expect all of them to end with pain and a throbbing headache?"

She looked skyward, thinking. "Probably, Robert."

"It's Dexter."

"Where?" she said, eyes skimming the room. When he closed his eyes and sighed again, she covered her mouth and stuffed back a laugh.

CHAPTER 13

The next morning Lainey resumed her fight against poverty by immersing herself in several new orders, including the ones Ian procured for her. The people she contacted had questions. She could tell by the way they said, "Oh, you're Ian's friend," as if wondering her connection to the notoriously lone wolf. Lainey remained demure for once, not bothering to assuage their curiosity and blurt more than she should.

It had been nice, that little break after her breakdown. She slept and rested and cleaned and cleared her head. That was how she knew marrying Dexter was the right thing, because she thought about it with a healthy brain for once. Not like all her other decisions that were usually fueled by emotional impulse and caffeine. Now, for instance, when she was on hour twenty-three of no sleep, would be the wrong time to make any major life decisions. Good thing for her she only had to finish her current order and then she was done.

Eventually she would have to decide how best to use the money Dexter was about to give her. Should she refuel her lagging savings account or buy a chocolate enrober? Having money in the bank was a good idea, obviously, but buying the enrober would save her hours and hours of work, could increase her productivity, probably tenfold.

Most of her tedious labor was spent tempering and dipping chocolate. The enrober would take care of both, potentially saving hours of effort. But outside of a vehicle it would be the most expensive thing she would ever buy. Could she justify that when her savings account was running on fumes? These were the times she wished she had someone to ask, a business mentor or friend who would know best how to help her. She thought of calling Murphy and quickly dismissed the idea. Clearly her brother didn't care, or at least not in the tangible way she wanted him to. She could call her dad but, given his history of bad decision making, he would probably tell her to take the money and buy magic beans.

Dexter came to mind, but she quickly discarded him. *I am not here to fix you.* Ouch, but point taken. Once again Lainey would have to figure things out on her own with no help. And she would, but not today.

At some point, she assumed it was evening but really had no idea, Dexter knocked.

"Stop knocking," she yelled.

"You want me to go away?" he said, poking his head around the door.

"No, I want you to stop knocking and walk in. Who does the knock benefit?" She didn't bother to look up, so engrossed was she in her task of unmolding and packaging tiny chocolate fire engines. She'd found a company that made molds to her specifications, and it had the potential to be life changing, at least from a business perspective.

"Someone who doesn't want to be shocked by your exposed girly bits," he said.

"I only make candy in the nude for special events," she returned.

"Like what?"

"St. Agatha Day, the festival of naked candy," she said.

"Why do I ask the questions?" Dexter asked. He came into the kitchen and paused a few feet from the table, hovering.

"Now what are you doing?" Lainey asked.

"Trying to figure out how to sit down without getting my clothes dirty," he said. Everything had smears or drops of chocolate on it.

"Decide right now: clean clothes or marriage in name only plus chocolate."

With a sigh he pulled out a chair and sat. Lainey arranged a few of the chocolates she'd been working on in a little line and slid them toward him. "Eat them in this order."

"Or what?"

"They won't taste right and your mouth will explode. In the bad way."

"Is there a good way for that to happen?" he asked.

"Try it and see," she said, resuming her task.

He ate the chocolates in the proper order and had to admit, if only to himself, that there was a bit of a taste explosion. Of course his fingers were also now covered in melty chocolate that hadn't fully hardened yet. By now he knew where the dishcloths were and helped himself, running it under warm water to try and clean himself off.

When he was reasonably clean, he realized Lainey had finished her project and was now apparently stuck, staring at her finished chocolates.

"Did you run out of gas?" he asked.

"I think maybe my battery unwound," she said.

"How long have you been up?"

"What year is it?"

He went forward and used the wet cloth to try and clean her, starting with her face and working downward. She blinked sleepily up at him, remaining patiently still like a sticky toddler while he wiped her cheeks and then attempted to clean her hands. When he realized her fingers were coated in too many layers of chocolate, he took her by the wrist and led her to the sink.

"Why no gloves?" he asked.

"Need to feel it to make sure it's right. Plus they get caked with chocolate. Gross."

"Indeed, that's disgusting," he said dryly, peeling back what had to be ten rings of chocolate from her thumb. It was like age-dating an ancient tree. "Lainey, you have to sleep."

"Sleep is for the weak," she returned, suppressing a yawn.

"You are weak," he reminded her when she swayed a little.

"Oh, then who is staying up for days and working for low pay for?" she asked, unable to suppress the yawn this time.

"The stupid," he said. "You work so much more efficiently when you're fresh and well-rested. Scientific studies have proven that…"

He stopped talking because she leaned against him and fell asleep, still standing like a horse, her cheek mashed flat against his sternum, lips puckered and half open. They flapped softly on each exhale like a party noisemaker that lacked enthusiasm for its job.

Why did I come here? he wondered. Why did he willingly subject himself to her calamitous life? He could have gone straight home, eaten supper, and watched TV on his couch. Instead he was playing the role of barn stall to her Mr. Ed. And yet he couldn't bring himself to wake her. Instead he bent and swept her into his arms, wincing when something pulled hard in his lower back. He was definitely going to feel this later, and she wasn't even awake to appreciate his selfless heroics.

He carried her to the couch and plopped down with a grunt, Lainey flopping, her head precariously close to smacking the arm of the couch. Unaware, she curled toward him and *nestled.* Apparently it came easier to her than to him. He slid an afghan over her and she snuggled impossibly closer.

Dexter looked around for something to do and spied a remote. Every night he came home, sat on the couch, and watched the news. Why? He had no idea. It didn't affect him or his world to know or understand what was happening in Europe, but there was something secure and settled about knowing anyway. He reached for the remote, inadvertently smashing Lainey beneath him, and turned on the TV. And then stared blankly at snowy fuzz.

Lainey, who must have come to when he smashed her, reached over her head and handed him a second remote.

"Thank you," he said.

"Mmm," she garbled.

"Does this count as my affectionate gesture for the day?" he asked, thinking it should count double if the pain in his back was any indication.

"Nuh-uh. This is just good manners." She poked his belly. "Do something else. Something sweet." The lip twitch was a good sign that she was enjoying his misery. And yet his hand seemed to have a mind of its own as it petted her head. Mostly it began as a way to get the stray hairs out of her eyes. How did that not drive her crazy? It made him itchy to be near it.

But when she made a little mewling sound of sleepy delight, his hand kept up its routine, long after the hairs were smoothed away from her face. Her hand crept out and tugged the hem of his shirt, wrapping it in her fist, and then she was out again.

You can stop petting her now, he reminded himself. But somehow he didn't. He smoothed his palm over her hair with a sudden understanding of why pets lowered blood pressure because, despite the daily dose of horror on the nightly news, Dexter felt calm and, dare he admit, happy.

The next day at work, Dexter saved the news as long as possible. Eventually he broke it to them.

"I'm taking the afternoon off."

Eight scowling Russian eyes looked up at him with so much accusation it was as if he'd announced he kicked their puppy down the stairs.

"What? Why? Where are you going?" Yuri demanded.

"Is other job. He is leaving us for other job," Maxim declared, thumping his fist on the table with a bang that made it rattle.

"Who are they? We will put curse on them," Andrei said.

"We should call Sonya. She knows all the good curses," Ivan agreed.

"It's not another job. It's an afternoon off. I take time off occasionally," Dexter said.

"Not since vacation two years ago," Yuri said. "Also that reminds me I have three hours of community service to finish."

Two years ago when Dexter took his last vacation, the brothers decided to stage a shirtless exhibition-wrestling match in the park in the middle of winter. Dexter had no idea how they accidentally destroyed a one-of-a-kind bronze statue, nor did he ever want to know. It haunted him enough that he hadn't taken off time since.

"I have to take the afternoon off. Lainey and I are getting our marriage license today."

Now they stared at him in a different way, one that was somehow more disconcerting than the overblown histrionics. "What?" he snapped when all of them remained unnervingly silent.

"Marriage license. Is big deal, Dexter," Yuri said.

Dexter shrugged. "It's a necessity for marriage. I'm getting married. I told you this."

"Yes, but then it was so…theoretical. Now is getting real. Are you sure you're ready for this?" Andrei piped in.

Dexter never enjoyed it when they tried to be the grownup in the relationship. He had gotten used to being the human Russian wrangler. He shook his shoulders, trying to toss off their concern. "It's fine. We're ready. We've settled everything."

"Settled…what?" Maxim drawled.

"The way it's going to be. We have a contract that spells out our expectations so things don't get messy."

"Is woman. Things will always be messy," Ivan said. The others nodded.

"It's not like that," Dexter said, trying hard to tamp down his annoyance.

"Not like what? What do you really know about this woman? Other than strange love of cherries in jar," Yuri said.

"Also good kisser," Andrei added helpfully, pointing at his brothers who nodded.

"Pretty," Maxim added helpfully.

"Not as pretty as Sonya," Ivan inserted loyally. The brothers nodded their furious agreement, darting glances in case their sister was somewhere nearby listening and waiting to put curses on them. Knowing Sonya, it wasn't outside the realm of possibility.

"It's not like that. Lainey's nice and she's going into this with her eyes wide open. It's not like she's going to hoodwink me and steal my kidneys."

They blinked at him. "Is that American wedding custom?"

"No, it's that old urban legend. You know, the guy goes to the party, gets drunk, and wakes up the next morning in a bathtub of ice without his kidneys."

"Why would party people steal his kidneys?" Yuri asked, still clearly believing this was some hidden facet of American life he hadn't yet discovered.

"They were med school students who sold his kidneys on the black market for a lot of money," Dexter explained.

The brothers perked up. "Kidneys sell for lots of money?"

Dexter jutted a finger, encompassing all of them. "Do not steal or sell any kidneys. And because I know how your minds work, this includes all other organs in the body."

"What if they're not in the body when we find them?" Ivan asked, raising his hand.

"No," Dexter said. "No trafficking body parts of any kind. It's the kind of illegal that will get you deported."

They deflated and sat back. The brothers had a line: good clean fun that would earn a slap on the wrist and bad enough to get them sent back to Russia. That seemed to be the only line they respected, that and their insane sister.

"What about a ring?" Ivan asked.

"You can sell a ring, if you find it. Not if you steal it," Dexter said, reaching for his coat.

Yuri tossed a coaster at him. It was marble and pinged painfully off his ribcage. "Not our ring, *bestolkovyy*. Your ring with girl."

"We're not getting rings because, again, it's not a real marriage," Dexter said.

They all did the silent staring thing again. He was really starting to hate that.

"What?" he asked, teeth gritted.

"We're beginning to wonder if you actually are the smart one," Ivan said.

"Dexter, women always want ring," Andrei said, nodding. "Take it from us, we have sister."

Dexter didn't point out that their sister actually would sell someone's kidney for jewelry. Not all women were like that, surely. Not about something that didn't even count. "It's *not* a *real* marriage."

"Why did you say it like that? With syl*lab*les all *slan*ted?" Maxim demanded.

"Must be nervous American thing," Yuri said, deftly catching the coaster when Dexter tossed it at his head on his way out of the room.

CHAPTER 14

Dexter had told Lainey to be ready at exactly fifteen minutes past noon. The courthouse was open until four, but he didn't like to cut things that close. Plus, knowing Lainey as he was beginning to, he thought she might need some wiggle room on the time. Call him crazy, but she seemed like the type of woman who was always late.

And when he arrived home and let himself into her darkened apartment, his fears were confirmed. Her car was there, so he knew she hadn't left. She must have fallen asleep again, which meant she would have to get ready, which meant he would have to tamp down his ire and impatience as he waited an unknown time for her, after he made a special point of leaving work early.

She wasn't in the main parts of the house. Since hers was a mirror of his, he followed the stairs to her bedroom and found her burrowed under the covers. With a lightning stab of annoyance he flicked on the light and stood at the edge of her bed.

"Lainey!"

She lay still a few beats, then flung off the blankets and beamed at him, fully dressed. "I tricked you."

"What?"

"You thought I wouldn't be ready. But look at me, all ready. Ta-da."

"Congratulations on being a functioning adult. Now let's go."

"Wait, how was your day?" she scooted over and patted the bed.

He perched on the edge of it and let out the breath he seemed to hold all day at work. "It was…you know. It was work."

"I don't really know anymore. I kind of miss working with people. I didn't see that coming."

"You could go back," he said.

She squinted up at him. "Could you lie down? Staring at the light behind you hurts my eyes."

He popped off his shoes and lay down, letting go of another breath as he stretched out. "Your bed is soft."

"Is yours an ironing board?" she guessed.

"Nails."

"Ah, figures. Back to your earlier statement, just because I miss people and routine doesn't mean I'm ready to give up yet. Feels like failure."

He didn't respond, but quitting his job to try some far flung dream, one that could and would only end in failure and, if looks were any indication, was already failing, was unfathomable to him. He needed the security of nine to five, of frameworked tasks, of money in the bank and viable retirement.

Lainey yawned and reached for the hem of his shirt, winding her fist in it.

"No," he said, yanking it away.

"What?" she asked, affronted.

"I know that move. You're about to fall asleep for real."

"I like to hold things when I sleep," she said. "Makes me feel cozy."

"Don't sleep, we have to go," he said, but he yawned. Her bed really was comfortable, soft and plush and *cozy*.

"Let's pretend for a minute."

"That we can get you out of here on time?" he said hopefully.

"No, that it's true. That we're really getting married," she said.

"I thought we are really getting married."

She poked him. "You know what I mean. We're crazy in love, can't keep our hands off each other." She stretched her arms around him and gave him a squeeze. "We sleep all night bundled like puppies because we're sooooo in *lurve*."

"No one actually sleeps that way," he mumbled. The weight of her warmth was dragging him under.

"Play along," she growled, squeezing harder.

He put his arms around her and she *nestled*, burrowing comfortably into his embrace, a perfect fit. "Oh, darling. I can't wait to argue about which way the flap on the toilet paper goes with you," she gushed.

"For the rest of our lives," he said, imitating her breathless dreaminess in a way that made her giggle.

"I love how you snore. When I can't sleep because you sound like a stuck chainsaw, I stare at you for hours, feeling so much love I want to die. Not like I want to stuff a pillow over your face and suffocate you at all."

"And when I'm trying to go to sleep and you keep talking and talking and talking and talking, I think to myself, 'how did I get lucky enough to find an incessant chatterbox who won't shut up'?"

She giggled and pressed her face to his chest and he smiled. And then somehow woke up an hour later, Lainey still molded firmly against him.

"Lainey," he whispered, giving her a shake. "Wake up, we fell asleep."

Her eyes flapped open. "Oh. Good nap, though."

It had been, actually. His alarm went off and she sat up. "Did you set your alarm for our impromptu nap?"

He pushed the button on his alarm. "I don't really do impromptu," he reminded her.

"Consistency is key," she said, touching her finger to his cheek. She turned to go, but he held her back.

"Wait I have to ask you something."

"Kind of anticlimactic. I already said I'll marry you."

He picked up her left hand and regarded it. "Do you want a ring?"

"I've had my eye on the Hope Diamond," she said.

He shook her hand.

She let out a little breath and also now stared at her hand, rather both their hands since they were still joined. "Maybe. Not a diamond or stone, but a little band might be nice. Sort of a reminder of our temporary commitment, you know? There's something kind of sweet and solemn about that."

"Yeah," he agreed, thumb smoothing over her ring finger. "How come no diamond? I thought girls liked that kind of stuff."

"A diamond is too real. Too—emotionally involved. It says you put thought and effort and energy into selecting something for me." She paused. "I don't think I'll ever have a ring like that. Not really."

She sounded so sad. He didn't like it. "Why not?"

She let go of his hand and bundled her knees to her chest, wrapping her arms around them. "I have this friend who is a firefighter." It still hurt too much to say Ian's name. "He told me about this tank they have that when they run out of water can go to any lake or river or pond or even swimming pool and suck up all the liquid. That's me, I'm that tank. I suck the life out of people, always require more than they have or are willing to give. And then I spew it back at them like an out-of-control hose, bowling them over with too much love, too much affection, attention."

"That's a terrible thing to say," he said.

"No, it's a truthful thing to say. I'm trying really hard to use this time to grow and improve and become better. And part of that is realizing that I'm the common denominator in every failed relationship. I alternately ask too much and give too much. In short, I am too much."

They were quiet a few beats. Dexter studied her with a thoughtful frown, but he couldn't disagree because maybe it was true. He didn't know, nor would he. It wasn't like they were in a real relationship. So far she'd been fun and funny and a little kooky, but he'd only scratched the surface. What if, beneath that, she actually was needy and a little insane?

She reached over and gripped his hand again. "Look, I know you said you're not a fixer, and I respect that. But maybe if you see things in me, things that are starting to tip over the margins, you could point them out. Like, 'Lainey, this is what you were talking about. This is you being too much.' And then *I* could fix them. Because I don't know when I'm doing it. I don't know until after it's already too late, until after I've pushed away all the people I care about." She sniffed and brushed at her eyes. "Please? Okay?"

"I'll try," he said slowly. "But I don't want to hurt you."

"I'll think of it as ripping off a Band-Aid. You're an unbiased observer. You can see all my rough spots that need to be polished. This could be like a master class in relationship prep." She wriggled, warming to her idea. "This could be amazing. Why doesn't everyone take a practice run at marriage? I see so many benefits looming in our future." She gave his hand a squeeze.

He smiled, glad she'd regained her sparkle. Lainey was a warm, passionate person. To see her without that warmth and passion, even temporarily, felt like a cold, gray drizzle.

"Clearly we're relationship geniuses," he agreed.

"Maybe we should write a book, when all of this is over."

"How To Marry Your Neighbor And Succeed At Life," he suggested.

"How To Be Opposite And Not Kill Each Other," Lainey added.

"Let's give that one time. We might have to amend it by the end," he said, checking his watch. "Speaking of which, can we pretty please go before the courthouse closes?"

"I'm waiting on you. I'm completely ready," she said, motioning to herself.

He quirked an eyebrow. "Really?"

"Just got to touch up my hair and makeup after the nap. Back in a tick." She hopped out of the bed and darted to the bathroom.

Sighing, Dexter picked up the book by the bed and started to read, some girly romance novel. Twenty minutes later, Lainey finally reappeared in the doorway.

"Are you ready yet? They're going to close," she said, hands on hips.

"Maybe a how-to manual," Dexter suggested as he eased out of the bed and tidied it behind him, pulling the sheets taut. "How Not To Kill The Stranger You Married."

"Might want to hold off on that. It might need to be amended by the end," she said. She reached around him, ruffled the sheets he'd perfected, took his hand, and dragged him out of the room before he could fix the bed again.

❦

*A*s the day wore on, their light mood slid toward solemnity. Things began to feel more real when they had to sign papers and fill out their marriage certificate application. Next they went to look at rings, and another realization jolted them as they viewed all the other happy couples picking out their forever rings.

"What can I show you?" an eager saleswoman asked as they stared dazedly at the ring counter.

"Something cheap and temporary," Dexter said, elbowing Lainey when she snorted a laugh.

"Something simple," he amended when the woman's eyes widened and swung sympathetically toward Lainey.

"Simple is good," Lainey agreed, rescuing him.

"Okay," the woman drawled, her hopes for a good commission dwindling. "Here are our simplest bands." She pulled out the tray and set it on the counter, not bothering to remain while they made their inspection.

"Kind of anticlimactic," Lainey said, picking up a ring that looked like all the others.

"Were you hoping it would shoot fireworks or something?" Dexter asked, picking up a matching band.

"No, although not going to lie, now that you said it I think it's a genius marketing idea. I just...Everyone makes it out to be such a big deal. The *ring*." She pressed her palm to her cheek. "But it's only a piece of metal." Her hand moved up and down a few times, feeling the weight of it.

"Try it on," Dexter urged. "Maybe it feels different on."

Dutifully, she slid it on her finger. Dexter did the same and they made a combined inspection. "Do you feel married?" he asked.

"No, but I feel a little weird, seeing something that should have meaning but doesn't. Do you think everyone feels this way?"

"Maybe no one overthinks it this much. Maybe they're too busy thinking about all the other stuff to give credence to rings," Dexter mused.

"Credence to rings is an excellent band name," Lainey said. She slid the ring off and set it on the counter. Dexter took his off and lined it next to hers.

"These?"

"These seem as good as any others," he agreed, nodding. They stared at them, side by side on the clear glass counter.

"Yep," she agreed. They couldn't seem to take their eyes off the rings, a tangible symbol of the reality they were about to undertake.

At last the saleslady rescued them with her return. They purchased the rings, shoved them deep into a bag, and went to get something to eat, deciding to get carry out when the wait was too long. Hanging around a restaurant endlessly felt too much like a date. Fast food felt more in line with the current theme of things—ill thought and laced with a touch of shame.

They sat on Lainey's couch as they ate, staring at the bag that contained their rings.

"Why did it feel so weird?" Dexter mused.

"Maybe it was the shock. We're really doing this. Maybe we need to put them on for a while, like practice. You know when you buy new shoes for a vacation but you have to break them in a few times so you don't get blisters when you wear them?"

He stared at her. "You know I'm a guy, right? We don't buy vacation shoes, and we don't calculate for blisters."

"Must be anarchy," she observed.

"Must be looking in a mirror," he muttered. "But it's not a bad idea, the practice ring thing." He finished his food and wiped his fingers with a napkin. Not that they needed it. Somehow he had remained clean while Lainey's fingers looked like she'd run them through a combo oil-slick/ketchup rain-wash. He used one napkin and handed the remainder of the stack to her. She used them all and shoved them in the bag.

Neither of them made a move toward the rings.

"Right, yes, being a man," Dexter said. With a definitive nod, he reached for the bag, pulled out his ring, and put it on. Nervously, Lainey took her ring and slid it on, too. They sat there staring at their respective hands in silence a few minutes.

"Not getting any less weird," Lainey observed.

"Can we take them off now?" Dexter said.

"Yes, but like brave adults," Lainey said. She demonstrated by sliding the ring gently off her finger and easing it back inside its box. When both ring boxes were in the bag, she tossed it onto the coffee table and wiped her hand on her pants.

"Brave. Adult," Dexter said, nodding.

"I need chocolate now," she replied, heading toward the kitchen.

"Do you ever not need that?" Dexter called.

"In different forms, based on my mood and life events. Today calls for the big guns. Dark and all its ensuing flavonoids." She returned and handed him a square of chocolate.

"One square? And it's not even shaped like a bunny or rolled around a cherry," he said, holding it aloft with a frown. In the short time he'd known her, he had come to expect better, in terms of candy.

"This is need-based chocolate. There are no medicinal bunnies. Just eat it." She bit off a hank using her molars, as if it were a medieval turkey leg and she was about to partake in a joust. Unable to participate in the primal display, he instead popped the whole thing in his mouth like a pill, letting it dissolve on his tongue. It did so nicely, far smoother than he would have guessed by its appearance. And maybe it was placebo, but he did start to feel better, calmer and more settled.

Lainey finished her piece and had to wipe her hands again. She also seemed far cheerier than she had a moment ago. "If rings don't make you married, what does? What does 'married' mean? Because so far we only know what it isn't. So what is it? What makes someone really married? It's not going to happen for us when we take the vows, we've already decided. If the vows don't make it so, and the rings don't make it so, what makes it real?"

"You sound like the velveteen rabbit," Dexter noted.

"I *feel* like the velveteen rabbit," Lainey agreed. She had spent all of her life feeling roughed up and unloved. Too much for some people, not enough for others.

"To answer your question, I have no idea. Luckily it's not a question that concerns us. Maybe by the time it happens to you for real, you'll figure it out."

"Doesn't it bother you? The not knowing?" she asked.

"Nope. I deal with more tangible things. Speaking of which, is there anyone you want to invite to the wedding?"

She wrinkled her nose. "No."

"Thanks for the rapid response and immediate disgust. Feels good," Dexter said.

"It has nothing to do with you and everything to do with them. My family isn't involved in my life, by choice. They moved away to Florida and seem happy to forget they have a daughter."

"Sorry," he said.

"Not to be a sad sack, but it seems to be the pervading consensus among everyone I know. We moved a lot when I was a kid, and I wasn't a pariah at each new school, but neither did I assimilate. I sort of orbited. I sat with kids at lunch, played with them at recess, and passed a few notes. But I was never invited to the play dates, the sleepovers, the parties." She reached for the fast food bag and began laboriously folding down the top of it in some intricate manner, smoothing it each time to make the creases perfect. "What about you? Where did you fall in the social hierarchy?"

He shrugged one shoulder. "The same place I always dwell. In the middle. I wasn't popular, not unpopular. Played some sports, wasn't a super athlete. Good manageable grades, wasn't a super brain."

She turned her attention from folding the bag to studying him. "You sound remarkably well-adjusted."

"I am. Sorry."

"I don't know how to be that way, okay with mediocrity. I've always aimed to be stellar, to dream big, to reach big. And then when I fail, as I inevitably do, I feel so devastated. Feels like I'm on a constant roller coaster. I kind of hate it, but I don't know how to get off. It's the same with my goals and with people. I want to achieve amazing things, I want big love. Neither ever happens. Lately it's getting harder to believe in both my dreams and people and I think, 'Is this how it happens?' Is this how people end up settling for a mediocre life in a mediocre marriage? Is that what I'm supposed to do? Should I go back to an office job that squeezes the life from my lungs, merely to provide a stable living? Should I settle with some schlub I don't hate when the love of my life might be just over the next horizon? All in all, it's very confusing to be a grownup."

"I suppose I view it differently," he said. She was relieved to hear no defensiveness in his tone, glad he realized she hadn't been alluding to him as the hapless schlub.

"How so?" she asked with genuine curiosity. When she was younger, she had always believed her way was best—big impossible, rose-colored dreams. But now that she'd had a big dose of reality, she was far more willing to consider other viewpoints.

"I like to feel like a productive member of society. It makes me feel like I'm doing my part to be a cog in the machinery, like I'm helping society and my family by being a willing participant. I'm repeating what my ancestors did before me, since the beginning of time. The continuity of that soothes me."

"Doesn't it feel…small to you? No offense."

He wasn't offended because he heard the sincerity in her tone, the seeking. She was trying hard to understand his point of view. It was a humble place to be, and he couldn't fault her for it, even if they disagreed. "No. What could be bigger than to keep all of society going? To repeat what's been done for thousands of years? I am a man, doing what men do. I wake up each morning and go to work at a job that challenges me, that brings me satisfaction. Someday I will marry —for real—and reproduce. And then I will teach my children to carry on the traditions I value and they'll become the cogs, doing the things on repeat that keep society going. That tangible connection to the past and the future, the sense of purpose in today, who could want more than that?"

She tipped her head, studying him, absorbing the words. "Maybe I envy you."

"You shouldn't, and neither should you emulate me. You know why?"

She shook her head.

"Because we're different, and that's okay. What works for me probably won't work for you, and vice versa. The trick is figuring out what works for you." He patted her knee.

She stared at the spot on her knee, still thinking. "That's good advice, and I appreciate it. But that doesn't count as your daily dose of affection."

"Oh, come on. That was me, reaching out, taking a step out of my comfort zone."

"My knee is outside your comfort zone?" she asked.

"So far I can barely see it," he said, squinting and shading his eyes as he stared at her knee.

"Who hurt you?" she asked.

He laughed. "No one, my family's not touchy-feely. We're worker bees, not whatever the opposite of that is. Are there cuddle bees? I don't think so."

"Why isn't your family touchy-feely? Don't you have a mom?"

"Of course I have a mom. I wasn't hatched in an incubator. My mom is Polish. She emigrated to Canada when she was in her twenties, met my dad who is an American, and moved down here. A couple of years ago after he retired, they moved back to Canada. But she's your typical Eastern European. She can be stern and stoic and, I suppose, cold. When I was little, she probably loved on me and cuddled me. But as I got older, I don't remember much of that. And, if we're being honest, I never missed it, never yearned for it. It was how it was, and to me that was normal. Gooey affection seems odder."

"But it's so important," Lainey said, tossing her arms wide in a sudden fit of passion. "There's nothing more important than touch. Don't make me tell you the sad monkey experiment."

"I'm familiar with the monkey experiment," he said. He remembered it from a psychology class, the poor baby monkeys who yearned for touch so much they ended up starving to death.

"And that doesn't haunt you?" she exclaimed.

"I'm not a monkey," he pointed out. "Maybe we fill our tanks in different ways."

That gave her pause. "What fills your tank, if not human contact?"

"I don't know. My tank feels perpetually full," he said.

"Freak," she murmured, and he laughed. Then she opened her arms. "Come here, I'm going to teach you affection, then you'll see what you've been missing."

Instead of going willingly into her arms, he shied away. "No, go away. It's too weird."

"It's in the contract," she reminded him, making a little come hither motion with her hands.

Sighing, he eased closer, allowing her to capture him and pull him close. His head rested on her chest, in what might have been a maternal gesture, if he had been thinking motherly thoughts just then, which he was not. Her hand began to pet his head.

"There, isn't that nice?" she murmured.

It was nice, but not for the reasons she probably hoped. She was soft and pretty and smelled good and Dexter had been away from dating for too long. He had tried to repeatedly tell himself she was off limits, but at the moment he couldn't remember why. He squirmed, trying to turn his thoughts away from her, but the motion upended them, plunging them backwards onto the couch with her beneath him.

"You go all in on hugs," Lainey said, voice muffled by his shoulder.

"This is not working," Dexter croaked. Was it warm in here? Why did the heat feel cranked up to eighty? "I am feeling the opposite of affection."

"Hatred?" she said, concerned as she began rooting from beneath him.

"I wish," he muttered. He eased to the side, lying next to her instead of on top, and that helped a bit. Her hair had become insistently messy with lots of flyaways now covering her face. Impossibly, she seemed not to notice them so he began smoothing them off and tucking them back, one by one.

"That," she said softly, swallowing hard. "That's affectionate."

"How so?" he asked. He was merely doing what needed to be done.

"Because you're taking care of me without thought, because it's what you do. You're the keeper of the hair. It's nice."

It was helping him forget the other stuff, the decidedly not-affection feelings he had recently felt, so he kept going, petting her head like a sleepy kitten. "It's not so bad," he agreed.

"That's what I've been trying to tell you," Lainey said.

She smiled. He smiled in return and realized, in that moment, that he liked her. It took him by surprise, that little fact. He had expected exasperation and responsibility to be his main reaction because they were his primary reaction to everyone. Most people made no sense to him. But, though they were vastly different, he got Lainey. She was warmth and sunshine and passion. All she wanted in return was the same. For her sake, he hoped someday she found it. Those things wouldn't happen with him, of course. He wasn't the passionate sort, was far too stodgy and settled for her. But they could do this. They could be friends who were kind to each other during a strange and complex interlude.

"One more week. Now is the time to sew any remaining wild oats," he said, his finger still skimming lightly over her face.

She gripped his arm and opened her eyes. "Oats sound so good right now."

"How can you want oats after cheeseburgers and chocolate?" he asked.

"Too late. You said it, and now it's happening." She sprang away from him, toward the kitchen.

"You're too highly suggestible," he called after her, suddenly cold at the loss of her warmth.

"A smart man would use it to his advantage," she returned.

And now he stared at the blank wall, trying and failing to come up with a reasonable response.

CHAPTER 15

A week later they were married. They had planned to go to the courthouse but, as usual, the Russians threw a cog in the machinery.

"No guests? No church?" Yuri said, personally affronted by the lack.

"It's not a real marriage. It's a quickie ceremony for legalities," Dexter reminded them.

"Yes, but…where is romance?" Maxim said. For a group of siblings who bickered constantly, they certainly agreed about almost everything.

"There's not supposed to be any romance because, see, it's not a real marriage," Dexter said.

"But…God," Andrei whispered, ducking the coming lightning bolt.

"Is not proper," Ivan chimed in.

Dexter had resisted squeezing the bridge of his nose for as long as he could. Now he did so, squeezing his eyes closed, too. "The wedding is tomorrow. I can't book a church and pastor on this short notice."

"Leave to us," Yuri said, rubbing his hands together.

"We will tell you when and where to show up. Is no problem,"

Andrei agreed. The remaining brothers nodded their agreement and Dexter knew it was pointless to argue.

"Fine," he said, defeated. The brothers traded triumphant glances that soon fled when they realized who was standing in the doorway. "Sonya," Dexter added in the same hopeless tone. He had managed to avoid Sonya since their last disastrous encounter. At the sight of her now, he had to suppress a shudder and the urge to pop another mint.

"We will go," Yuri said, eyes darting furiously for escape. Though they were exponentially larger, all of them cowered in the face of their sister's withering glare.

"Stay, goon squad," she said, to the relief of Dexter and combined disappointment of the others. "This is business. Though maybe Dexter and I will have time for pleasure after." She tossed him a coolly threatening stare. He tried not to wince and squirm with gathering dread.

Sonya sank gracefully into a chair, crossing her perfectly sculpted legs. As far as Dexter knew, she had never worked out a day in her life. Rather she was one of those rare people preternaturally gifted with both unbearable beauty and a pristine figure.

"So," she began. Even before she spoke, she had the men's captivated attention. She was one of those women, the magnetic sort who drew all eyes and ears. "We have problem."

The Popovs liked to use dramatic pauses as much as they enjoyed dramatic screaming and physical signs of machismo. Dexter waited her out but when it became clear she wouldn't speak again until prompted, he spoke.

"What?" He was more than a little wary that whatever she was up to had something to do with his wedding, but she soon dispelled that notion.

"While you boys have been playing love connection with Dexter and girl, we've gained a competitor."

"Bah," Yuri said, waving a hand. "Competitor. Who can compete with us? Is nothing. Is gnat to giant cow."

"Maybe. But soon could be entire colony of gnats that will devour cow," Sonya proclaimed and once again the men were silent.

"Who?" Dexter asked.

"A new company, fresh from Hungary."

Andrei hissed. In the litany of things The Russians detested, other Eastern Europeans ranked near the top.

"They can't gain on us," Maxim declared, banging a fist. "They couldn't possibly. There are five of us. We are Russian. And we have Dexter."

"Do we?" Sonya quirked a perfectly shaped brow at him. "Dexter seems awfully distracted lately. By *love*."

Dexter didn't reply because not only was he not in love, he knew for certain this part of things was merely Sonya's possessive jealousy. Silence was his only weapon, and it was formidable. When he failed to make a reply, she gave a pouty "tsk" in his direction and refocused on her brothers. "I am telling you, this is competition. Is trouble."

"What should we do?" Ivan asked, splitting the question between Dexter and his sister.

"I know arsonist who…" Sonya began, but Dexter held up a hand, cutting her off.

"We do nothing. We keep being excellent and let our reputation speak for itself. We are the number one restaurant supply business on the east coast, soon to be number one on the west coast, as well. We keep our heads down and ignore the so-called competition. And we keep our noses clean." He eyed all the Popovs, including Sonya who still looked mutinous over the rebuff of her arson offer. Or perhaps the rebuff of so many other things.

"Dexter is right," Yuri said at last with a nod. "We are best. Let Hungary try to catch up. We will devour them." He smashed his meaty fist into his other meaty palm and ground it back and forth.

Reassured, the other brothers moved on to a new topic—the extreme superiority of Moscow to Budapest. But Sonya remained focused on Dexter, eyebrow still arched in what could either be challenge or warning. In Sonya's case, it was probably both.

*L*ainey stared at herself in the mirror. A bride. Obviously none of it was going according to plan. Her family wasn't here, nor did they even know about it. She wasn't marrying Ian, as she had thought she would since she was thirteen years old. Ian was far away, if not physically then definitely emotionally. They hadn't talked since her bombshell announcement, nor would they. If there was one thing she knew for certain about Ian, it was that he couldn't handle the difficult emotions of life. It was why he didn't want to settle down, now or possibly ever. He ran from the hard stuff in life with the same tenacity he ran toward buildings that were on fire. It was uncanny, when she thought about it, how a man could be both so physically brave and emotionally fragile.

But today wasn't about Ian. It was about the near stranger Lainey was about to marry. What did she know about Dexter, really? Not nearly enough, not enough to marry him for real. He was straight laced and buttoned down, but not lacking a sense of humor. He was much too reserved with physical affection, almost skittish when it came to giving and receiving hugs. He was nice. Settled. *Normal.* Previous to this moment, those things would have triggered Lainey's gag reflex. She wanted adventure! Passion! Romance! The very last thing she wanted was a normal, average guy who doled hugs like Hanukah gvelt, once a year for special occasions. But now that she was here and about to take the plunge, she felt an odd sort of peace. Dexter was *kind.* He was *loyal.* He was *there,* so very there. He was the sort of person who would take care of you, if you ever got sick. He had carried her to the couch when she fell asleep on him. How many times had he covered her with an afghan? He even washed her towering mound of dishes, and not because he was trying to make a good impression, but merely because it was the sort of person he was. He was a doer, a worker bee. Until she became friends with him, Lainey had no idea how comforting it would be to have someone like that in her life.

She was from a family of dreamers. Even her emotionally unavailable brother, Murphy, lived in the clouds, in his way, always more enamored with the possibility of a new venture than the actual work it took to get there. Just like their dad. *Just like me,* she thought and quickly quashed it. She was not like them. She was killing herself to prove otherwise. For goodness sake, she was marrying a stranger for the sake of keeping her business afloat. *If that doesn't say stability... Wait, no, that actually says the opposite...*

Once again she cut off the flow of her thoughts and focused on her reflection, tucking a stray hair, patting smooth a tiny imperfection in her eye shadow.

Someone knocked on the door to the room she was using and opened it before she could answer. "Lainey, are you ready? It's time." Dexter swung the door wide and stood in the entryway, blinking at her. "Wow, you look..."

"Not a complete and total disaster like usual?" she asked. She had put effort into her appearance today, great effort. She felt like she sort of owed him, for all the times he'd had to wipe strawberry sauce off her cheek and push the escaped hairs out of her eyes. She may not have much to offer, but she could look good, when she wanted. Today she wanted.

Dexter smiled. "I wasn't going to say that. You look pretty, are pretty." He came forward and stood beside her, watching both of them in the mirror.

She sighed, exasperated. "You're supposed to put your arm around me." As for her, she rested her head on his shoulder. They looked good together, in the mirror. As if they fit somehow, which must be a trick of the lighting and fancy clothes because of course they didn't. They couldn't be more opposite.

"I didn't want to touch you and mess it all up," Dexter said. Dutifully, he slid his arm around her waist and rested his head against hers.

"The only way to mess it up is to not touch me. Spoiler alert: I liked to be touched."

"You're kidding," he intoned. "If only you had told me once or ten thousand times."

"And yet I have to keep telling you," she said, nudging him.

"I'll try to do better," he promised, kissing the top of her head.

She smiled. "You're off to a good start."

"You ready to do this thing, Future Fake Wife?"

"Yes, but after the ceremony are you going to start calling me Present Fake Wife?"

"I could really toss a ringer in there and start calling you Past Participle Future Ex Wife," he said.

She giggled. "You're diabolical. To answer your question, yes. I am ready. How are my men of honor? Are they ready?"

The Russians had divided themselves in half, two best men for Dexter, two men of honor for Lainey, despite the fact that neither had asked them to participate. But it seemed important to them and, as they were the ones who found the church and pastor last minute, Lainey and Dexter made no objection. Really, it was kind of nice not to have to stand up alone, even if the alternative was four glowering Russians.

"They were born for this moment," Dexter said. "Also every moment before and after. They're really live-in-the-moment kind of people."

"At one point I thought that was my dream guy," Lainey said, allowing him to clasp her hand and lead her out of the room.

"And now?" Dexter asked.

"Now I have no idea about anything," Lainey said, but cheerfully. It was hard to be sad in a wedding dress, she realized. Even if she didn't feel married (or about to be), she felt pretty. Maybe even beautiful. It was as if the dress gave her some kind of ethereal glow, the sort that otherwise would have been fueled by love. Maybe that explained why a bride could look so radiant on the day and walk away from her new husband a month later with no explanation. Because, as with the rings, being *married* had nothing to do with the rings or the dress or any of the other trappings of the day.

Then what is married? Lainey's inner voice asked. It was the same voice that remained mute when she needed to make a major life decision but sprang to life and decided to become a philosopher after the fact. Like now, when she was standing at the front of an unknown church, in front of an unknown pastor, the filling in an oversized Russian sandwich, about to marry her neighbor.

Shut up, we're doing this, Lainey told the voice.

This is how you wind up in trouble, the voice tried.

Too late, Lainey told it.

And then she became aware of a new voice, a real one outside her head. A woman had slipped into the back of the church and was now loudly weeping. Lainey turned to survey her, along with everyone else. She was dressed head to toe in black, including a veil that did nothing to obscure her stunningly beautiful visage.

"Friend of yours?" Lainey whispered to Dexter.

He shook his head, his expression looking pained and long-suffering.

She leaned closer. "Tell me one thing: It's not your mom, is it?" She could contend with a lot. Maternal disapproval wasn't on the list.

Smiling now, he shook his head. "Ignore it. I'll tell you later." He squeezed her hand. Reassured, she squeezed back and faced forward, and that was it. Despite the copious and dramatic weeping that was somehow placed to pick up the acoustics and echo all through the church, despite the fact that this was likely the worst decision she'd ever made, despite everything Lainey married Dexter. And it seemed as if everything would be okay.

And then one of the brothers clapped his hands together and loudly boomed. "Is time for honeymoon," and the woman at the back of the church gave way to a howl of rage before falling over gracefully in a dead faint.

CHAPTER 16

"As far as weddings go, that was a ten," Lainey declared. It was hours later, and they were on her couch, which had somehow become their ubiquitous go-to place.

Dexter laughed and squeezed the bridge of his nose. "I'm sorry. Honestly, it never occurred to me how many ways The Russians would hijack my wedding. In retrospect, it probably should have."

"Hey," Lainey said, resting her hand reassuringly on his forearm. "I was teasing you. I kind of loved it. It had everything—drama and humor and fainting. It was like watching a play where I was unwittingly the star."

He groaned some sort of guttural sound and swiped his hand over his face a few times.

"Who was the mysterious woman in black? Someone you used to date?"

"No," he said, dropping his hand and speaking with so much vehemence she jumped. "Sorry. Touchy subject."

"Normally I wouldn't pry…"

He gave her a look.

"Obvious lie. Of course I would. You have to tell me. I'm dying of curiosity overload. I have fatal Curious George disease and only you have the cure."

"It's not that I'm averse to telling you. It's...well, it's so embarrassing."

She didn't reply, merely kept staring at him, waiting.

He took a breath. "I've never told anyone before. It's harder than I thought it would be. The woman in black is Sonya, The Russians' sister. When I first started at the company, Sonya saw me and agreed in her own mind I should be her next conquest. Except I didn't respond, mostly at first because I don't mix business and pleasure. I was brought in because The Russians were volatile. Dating their beloved sister would only have added to that unstable combo."

He paused and she gave him an encouraging nod, eyes wide with rapt attention. To him the story was equal parts mundane and awkward, but she seemed to find it fascinating.

He took a breath and forged ahead. "Needless to say the rejection didn't go well. It's not something that happens to her often, maybe something that has never happened before. You couldn't see her well, but she's..."

"The most beautiful woman on the planet. I could tell, even through the veil and sobbing. But what's the part you're leaving unsaid? In what way did she not handle rejection well? What did she do?"

"She..." he paused again and looked at her. Why was it so hard to say the words? His face must be magenta, and he wasn't even the blushing sort. Inside he felt all squeamish and uncomfortable. He cleared his throat and looked anywhere but at her. "She started showing up unexpectedly, trying to pin me down, usually quite literally. She groped me, kissed me, threw unwanted advances at me." He braced for her laughter, but it didn't come. And when he chanced a peek at her face, it wasn't smiling. Instead her mouth was open, eyes wide in...sympathy?

"Dexter, that's terrible," she breathed, reaching out to grasp his forearm with both hands.

"It is?" he said, the words whooshing out of him like a long-held breath.

"Why wouldn't it be?" Lainey asked.

"Because she's a woman and I'm a man and on every conceivable scale she's leaps and bounds above me."

"She's a superior in a position of power and has been using it to harass you. She embarrassed you, made you feel uncomfortable and powerless. That's *terrible*," she reiterated. "I've never been harassed that way, but I see how it can make you feel objectified, how it can cause extreme anxiety, never knowing when or where she's going to strike. You must feel on edge all of the time."

"I do," he agreed slowly. He had expected amusement and derision, if he ever told anyone. *Have you seen her? Harass me, baby. Harass me all you want.* Her sympathy left him feeling almost woozy with relief. She believed him. She understood. Far from being delighted to receive attention from such a beautiful woman, he felt stressed almost to his breaking point and, yes, objectified. Sonya didn't want him for any reason specific to him; she wanted him because he was male and had said no. He let out another slow breath and felt the tension and anxiety drain out of him. All this time, this was what he had needed, for one person to believe and affirm him. "Thank you."

"Hey," she said, easing closer to put her arms around him and rest her head on his shoulder. "What are fake wives for if not to help with real problems? I'm here for you. And if you want me to have a talk with her, I will."

He laughed, imagining how that would go. Sonya would eat Lainey for breakfast and the thought was painful on a number of levels. He felt protective of Lainey, he realized, more than as a friend or neighbor. Even if it was in name only, she was his wife now. Nothing should happen to her on his watch.

"Why are you laughing?" she asked, giving him a squeeze.

"Sonya is crazy. I don't want you near her."

"Sorry to break it to you, but I'm my own brand of crazy. Clearly you have a type. And sometimes the only way to fight crazy is with crazy."

"It's enough that you know and you believe me," he said, resting his head on hers. Really, it was everything.

"The offer's on the table," she said in a chilling impression of a mafia don.

"I'll keep that in mind," he said. "Hey, doesn't this count…"

"No, this does not count as your daily dose of affection. Seriously." She let him go and gave him a little shove.

"I could kiss you again," he offered. He had kissed her at the end of the wedding, for tradition but also for something else. He hadn't been able to stop thinking about the first kiss. It shook him, that kiss, much more than he was willing to admit. He wanted to know if a follow up would be the same. So far he hadn't had time to dissect it and analyze if that were so. But based on the amount he wanted to kiss her again and keep kissing her, he feared so. "I like kissing," he said, more to himself than her. That was all this was, not a particular attraction to Lainey but an attraction to kissing in particular. He had always liked kissing, and he had never confessed it to anyone because he never heard any other guys say the same. Guys were supposed to like all the stuff that came after. Kissing was supposed to be for women. But Dexter had always enjoyed making out, merely for the sake of making out.

"Kissing isn't affection," Lainey declared.

"What? Why not?"

"Because it's a truck stop on the way to paradise."

He quirked an eyebrow at her, smiling when she blushed and shoved his shoulder. "You know what I mean. It's not a means to an end."

"It could be," he insisted.

"But it's not. It never is. Even if it starts out with good intentions, eventually it always leads somewhere, if you do it enough. And somehow you always pick up where you left off, never starting over at the beginning again. And we agreed…"

"Yes, we agreed," he interrupted before she could get cranked up. "If kissing is not affection in your mind, what is? Because clearly my education on the subject is lacking and I still don't understand."

"Affection is kindness using touch. It gives, it doesn't expect in return. It's reaching out to bestow gentleness on your person, merely because they're your person and not because you want something from them. It's hugging."

"I'm not a hugger," he said. It felt like too much to hug all the time; it felt like giving pieces of himself away that he wasn't ready or available to give.

"It doesn't have to be a hug. It can be a pat." She patted his knee. "A touch." She pressed her palm to his cheek. "You could hold my hand." She gave his hand a squeeze. "You could put your arm around me." She wriggled closer until he settled his arm on her shoulders. "You could even do both arms," she urged, nudging him. Dutifully, he added the other arm. She faced him and slipped her arms around his waist.

"Lainey, this is hugging," he said.

"Shh, no it's not. This is totally different," she said.

"You're nestling," he accused as she burrowed against him. "You're a shameless hug seeker."

"I love hugs, Dexter," Lainey declared in an impassioned tone, slightly muffled by her face against his chest. "If someone invented a device so I could hug someone all the time while still continuing to work, I'd say shut up and take my money."

"But…" he began, but she interrupted.

"It's our wedding night. Can't you let me have this? Somewhere out there a crazy Russian woman is probably trying to buy plutonium in order to kill me. This might be my last hug."

"So dramatic," he whispered, but he didn't refuse her. He told himself it was because it was, in fact, their wedding night and a hug was the least he could do. But really he started not to mind so much anymore. Lainey was snuggly soft and warm and she smelled incredible, a potent combo of chocolate, vanilla, and something girly. When she clutched his shirt in her hand, he thought she was falling asleep, but instead she used it to give him a little shake.

"I almost forgot. I have a gift for you, a wedding gift."

"What? Lainey, no." Dexter felt terrible; he hadn't gotten her anything. It never occurred to him, though it probably should have, given Lainey's warmth and propensity toward all things cozy.

"You're going to love it. Hold on." She hopped off the couch and skittered away, returning a moment later with a large ornately bedecked gift bag.

"Lainey," he said, longsuffering with self-recrimination. Why was he the type of schlub who didn't give hugs or gifts? His mother was good, great even, but why couldn't she have been the sort who bestowed warm gooey affection at every turn, thereby prepping him for someone like Lainey. In comparison, he felt like an East German guard at Checkpoint Charlie. He took the bag slowly, almost dreading to see inside. What if it was something really thoughtful, like a new dress shirt in the perfect size she somehow miraculously knew? But when he put his hand in the bag and withdrew the gift, he laughed in delight, holding it up to make a better inspection.

"It's us," she said, unnecessarily so because of course it was. She had created a bride and groom out of chocolate, a door between them. They each rested on the door, her smiling cheerfully, him looking somehow both reserved and exasperated.

"This is incredible, how did you do this?" He couldn't stop staring at it, turning it around and around to take in every perfect angle.

"I found a company that makes custom molds. There probably won't be a lot of people clamoring for sculptures that look exactly like us, but you never know." She sat on her hands, squirming with delight over his reaction. "Do you like it?"

He shifted it to his left hand and used his right to give her an impromptu hug. "I love it. It's the best, thank you."

"You're welcome," she said, grabbing his shirt and nestling again before he could think about letting go. It was only later that he realized the thought of letting go hadn't occurred to him.

CHAPTER 17

"So. Is big married man now. Probably thinks he is superior," Yuri declared, glowering at Dexter over the conference room table. They were supposed to be having their weekly status meeting, but apparently they had to get this out of the way first.

When Dexter first started with the Popovs, he tried to appease them. *Of course marriage hasn't changed me. Of course I don't feel superior to you.* He quickly realized it didn't matter. They could both advocate hard for his marriage and resent it at the same time. It was in their nature to always find the angst and contention in everything.

"If you say so," he said mildly.

Diffused and appeased by his blandness, they sat back, still staring at him. "What is marriage like, really? Is epic love?" Maxim asked.

"You know it's not," Dexter said. "We married for the sake of the party. We've been over this."

"Seemed like real love to us," Ivan pointed out.

Anything but a screaming, yowling catfight would seem like true love to them, Dexter reasoned. "Lainey's nice," he said.

"Maybe too nice," Andrei said.

Dexter's head snapped up. "What? She is not too nice. She's perfectly nice."

Apparently he'd fallen into some kind of trap because now all the brothers were grinning at him. "Oh, is nice, is she? Spoken like a man in love."

Dexter sighed. He was going to have to break out the big guns. He opened his briefcase and set out the chocolate sculpture Lainey had made for him. The brothers stared at him, confused.

"What is for?" Yuri asked, his Cro-Magnon brow lowered like the first person to encounter live fire.

"Lainey made it."

"Why?" Ivan asked.

"For a wedding present."

"Is giant chocolate. I am not seeing the point. Why must Americans make things so large? Chocolates should be small and shiny, like truffles," Maxim declared.

"It's us," Dexter said, pushing it closer.

"Lainey made sculpture of us?" Andrei asked.

"Not us, *us*. The people who are married to each other." He fought a shudder at hearing himself say it out loud. Married. Him. To a stranger. Yikes.

"Ah," Ivan said. Dexter fought another cringe as one of his meaty paws picked it up to make an inspection. "Is good. Look, she got Dexter's expression correct." He turned the sculpture toward his brothers who all guffawed in a unified chorus.

"Is clever girl, Lainey," Yuri said, darting Dexter a raised eyebrow.

"What?" Dexter said, pressing his thumb between his eyes.

"Is convenient, no? Girl in food business marries man in restaurant supply business," Yuri said. The other brothers lost their smiles and regarded Dexter in suspicion.

"Are you honestly proposing that Lainey set this up in order to tap into my vast family discount, one which I have never once used in all the years I've worked here?" Dexter said.

"Think about it," Andrei urged, tapping his temple.

"How far back did her diabolical plan start? Did she target the apartment next to mine, knowing I had access to Belgian chocolate?

Did she show up at the bar coincidentally when I needed an out with The Bristol?"

The brothers nodded. "You cannot trust American women. They are too nice. You should find good Russian girl who will rip out still beating heart to your face," Ivan said. "No surprises."

"I'm not finding anyone," Dexter said. "I have Lainey. I mean, I don't *have* Lainey, but I'm married to Lainey. For the foreseeable future and in the most technical sense." He tugged his collar. Was it hot or was he having a heart attack from the mass amount of stress he'd been stockpiling?

"Oooh," Maxim said, rubbing his hands eagerly together. "Is good to see Dexter squirm, yes?"

"Can we get back to work?" Dexter said.

They did so, because the brothers liked to work, but a short while later they were interrupted again, this time by a bike courier who delivered a package. Dexter usually hated interruptions, but in this case he was thankful. Anything to change the subject away from Lainey. It wasn't Lainey specifically he didn't want to dwell on, merely any further association between her and The Russians. He wanted to keep the two worlds separate, as much and as long as possible.

He signed for the package and squinted, straining to read the illegible print.

"What is?" Ivan asked.

"I have no idea," Dexter said. He opened the package, which contained a smaller package wrapped in plastic. He took that out, opened it, and had immediate regrets when the most putrid smell he'd ever encountered filtered out and filled the room.

Fighting his gag reflex, he instinctively slapped his hand over his nose.

"Is borscht?" Maxim asked, standing to get a better look.

"No, is rotten fish," Ivan exclaimed.

Dexter dropped his hand, using both to re-wrap the fish. Too late, though. The smell was everywhere. Before this moment he would have said he had a cast iron stomach, but this was testing his limits. Never had he smelled something so terrible.

"Who would have done this?" Andrei wondered, but his other brothers filled in the blank, shooting to their feet in outrage.

"Of course we know who."

"Is Hungarians."

"There's no proof," Dexter said, a task made more difficult because he was also holding his nose.

"Let me see box," Yuri said, snatching it away. "A-ha. Is Hungarian handwriting. Would recognize anywhere."

"How would you recognize Hungarian handwriting?" Dexter asked. "That's completely illegible and smeared."

"Because is cowardly and tainted with the blood of First World War," Yuri said, shaking it over his head in outrage.

"It's not Archduke Ferdinand's fish," Dexter said. He tried to keep his tone calm and even, but it was a losing battle. The Russians were gearing up for blood.

"We should send them dead cat," Andrei said.

"You cannot kill a cat," Dexter said, now shooting to his feet to match their indignation. Not that he could or even wanted to.

"Would not kill cat, obviously," Andrei said, waving his hand in dismissal. "Would find one already dead on side of road."

"No, send live cat with live rat and have it kill it on arrival," Ivan suggested.

"How could you possibly keep the rat alive until the precise moment?" Dexter inserted.

"No, send Sonya in box," Maxim said, warming to the subject. "Then Hungarians will be rats."

"What about that guy from the old neighborhood with stumpy pinky finger?" Ivan suggested. "Didn't rat chew that off? He might know way to train rat."

"He went against the Albanians," Yuri said, pressing his hand over his heart in a moment of silent respect.

Andrei snapped his fingers. "We could hire The Albanians."

"No," Dexter said, waving his hands like he was directing a plane on a freighter to try and get their attention. "We are not involving any more Eastern Europeans in our turf war. Yuri, Ivan, Maxim, Andrei, you are businessmen. In America. You are not thugs and lowlifes. You have a reputation here."

"Yes, for getting even," Yuri said, grinding his fist into his palm.

"No, for being professionals," Dexter countered.

"People think we are hitmen?" Ivan chimed in, perking up.

"Not that kind of professional. Professional businessmen. Respectable. Remember? We do things on the up and up. This," he pointed to the fish box, "is amateur hour. They're doing it because they're intimidated by your success. We take the high road, we rise above, we ignore them and don't give them the time of day. Why? Because we can't even see them from where we are. If other companies want to act like schoolboys, let them. The Popovs are *men*."

The brothers glanced at each other uncertainly. "Maybe Sonya…" one of them began. Dexter cut him off so quickly he didn't have time to see who it was.

"No. Absolutely no. We're men. We handle this like men. We rise above and play it clean and straight." For emphasis, he dusted his hands together. "Men. Yes?"

"Okay, men," Yuri agreed. He gave his hands a few halfhearted passes against each other and the other brothers followed suit. Dexter didn't have a lot of faith it would hold off the vengeance and bloodlust, but for now he'd take it.

*D*exter was exhausted by the time he let himself into Lainey's that night. He didn't question the fact that her side of the house was his first stop. *Duty or something,* he vaguely murmured to himself as he opened the door and took a breath, letting the weight of the day slip off him as he let it out.

As ever, her house smelled like chocolate, vanilla, and fruit but something more, something he couldn't identify. Whatever it was, it filled him up with a peaceful sort of feeling he hadn't felt since he was a kid, so he pushed that thought away, too.

"Lainey," he called.

"Come in the kitchen," she called.

He smiled at the anticipation in her tone. This was probably why people had dogs, so something would look forward to their arrival. It was nice, that. "Hey, what's up?" He entered the kitchen and saw Lainey beaming at him, arms outstretched in a poor attempt to hide something behind her.

"Guess what I bought?"

His jaw dropped, momentarily speechless.

"You don't know what it is," she guessed.

He did know what it was, but he couldn't believe she'd bought it. "Why?" he breathed.

"Why? It's an enrober. This saves me so much time, you have no idea. I just quadrupled my productivity. Probably more, but I don't know any math numbers bigger than quadruple."

"I know what it is, I don't know why you bought it," he said.

"I told you." She finally took in his gobsmacked expression. "What is the problem? Why do you care? You didn't specify what to do with the money you gave me. This is what I wanted it for." She pointed to the machine now taking up most of her kitchen counter.

"Oh, Lainey," he said, walking forward to make a slow inspection. "Don't you know who I work for?"

"The Russians," she said uncertainly.

He faced her, reaching out to tug the hem of her shirt. "I work for the Popovs."

She blinked, dazed. "The Popovs? As in Popov Restaurant Supply?"

He nodded.

Her mouth puckered in a silent O.

He eased closer and rested his forehead on hers, whispering, "I get a forty percent family discount."

"No," she gasped.

He nodded, using the motion to kiss the tip of her nose. "Can you take it back?"

"No returns," she said.

"No returns? That stinks. Where'd you get it?"

"I don't know, some new place running a bunch of deals. I think they're Hungarian," Lainey said, smiling when he barked a harsh laugh.

His hands rested on her hips. "If you need anything else, please tell me first."

"You said you weren't here to fix me," she reminded him.

"You are, in the most technical and legal sense, my wife. You can use my discount."

"Okay. Thank you." She slid her arms around him, resting her head on his heart. "How was your day?"

"It was a day," he said. "How about you? Anything more exciting than the enrober happen?"

"No."

"Wanna go out? I'm starved," he said.

"I made supper," she said, easing away to make a renewed inspection of her new appliance.

"You what?" he said.

She twirled to face him. "Why shocked? I cooked."

"Where is it?"

She pointed to the oven, the apparent source of the good smells.

"You cooked for me?"

"I cooked for us. Is that not okay? Did you have your heart set on going out?"

He shook his head. "No one cooks for me."

"I cooked for you. I gave you pot roast," she reminded him.

"You gave me leftovers. Don't get me wrong, they were great. But you cooked for me. I think maybe this is my version of your hug love. Food, Lainey, food." He tapped his fist over his heart.

"Okay," she said, pressing her palm to his cheek. "Oh, hey, I have something else for you."

"Lainey, no, you don't have to get me anything," he protested but inside he perked up. What would it be this time? A life-size chocolate pony? There was an inner child somewhere hoping that was the case.

"Don't get too excited. It's something I found." She led the way to her closet in the entryway and stepped inside.

"If a talking lion greets us, we're leaving," Dexter said, smiling when she laughed.

The closet was deeper than it looked. She disappeared into its recesses, Dexter close behind, shifted aside some coats and pointed in triumph. "Ta-da."

"It's a door," he blurted.

"Wow, you *are* smart," she said. "I bet there's one in your closet that connects."

"I bet you're right. How did I never notice that before?" he said.

"You weren't looking. It's hard to see things unless you're searching," she said.

"Wise wife," he said, reaching out to touch a wisp of her hair. She responded by standing on her toes and kissing him, a kiss that almost knocked him off his toes. And then she let him go and took a step back with a little laugh.

"Sorry. That was probably a mixed signal. But we're in a closet and I suddenly had this flashback to middle school where cute boy plus closet equaled kissing and…" she stopped talking, probably because he grabbed her and kissed her.

And despite the fact that he grabbed her, the kiss was soft and gentle, or at least it started out that way. Lainey made a little gasping sound that pushed him over the edge. He picked her up, mashing her into the clothes behind her as he deepened the kiss. She followed, plunging her fingers into his hair and grasping him with what seemed to them both like desperation.

It wasn't the sort of kiss that could stay in the closet, but before Dexter could take a step outside, his phone rang and he froze.

"The Russians?" Lainey asked, lips moving whisper soft against his.

"The Russians couldn't stop this. It's my mom, and I have to take it." Was he…was he panting? Mortifying.

She seemed not to notice as she slid out of his grasp and failed to right her toppled messy bun. "Kay," she replied, tucking her hands safely behind her back. So she wouldn't reach for him again? He'd have to ponder that later.

"Hi," he said, sliding his thumb across his phone as he brought it to his ear. Then he covered the mouthpiece and spoke to Lainey. "I'm going to go open it on my side."

She nodded, smiling. "Don't say hi to your mom for me," she whispered and he stifled a snort laugh.

"Nothing, I was laughing at something else. How's Dad?" He walked out of the closet. Lainey remained staring at her variety of winter coats. She shook her head, trying to snap out of her trance. *What happened here?* She'd kissed Dexter on a whim, for a spot of fun. The end result had been anything but fun; instead it had been rather earth shattering. What happened? Why did she respond to him that way? It was Dexter. She wasn't attracted to him. Was she?

Maybe the closet is magic, her handy brain suggested.

Yes, that must be it. It was the closet, nothing more. By the time he reached his side and opened the door, she stood at the edge, safely out of reach. He smiled and waved, pointing to his door in triumph. She smiled, tossing him a little wave. He winked and she fled to the kitchen, putting distance between herself and the magic closet of inevitable doom.

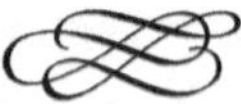

CHAPTER 18

They didn't kiss again, and neither mentioned it. Somehow they had an unspoken agreement that it had been a closet-related blip and nothing more. Instead they settled into a happy, remarkably domestic routine. On the days Lainey didn't have a big order, she cooked supper. When she was stuck for hours working, Dexter picked up takeout and spent the remainder of the evening helping her with whatever she was doing. She was always appreciative of those times, overtly so, no matter how many times he told her he enjoyed it. He liked the change of pace from his job, the part that allowed him to turn off his brain and stir or dip or wash things on repeat. But it was more than that; he enjoyed spending time with Lainey, even when she was stressed out and overly tired, she was fun and pleasant company, lighting his world with her quick wit and warmth.

And so somehow, without notice by either of them, they began spending all Dexter's non-working hours together, including every weekend. Neither knew when or how it morphed to an assumed, nor how they slowly began speaking in the plural. *What are we going to do this weekend?*

If they privately acknowledged this phenomenon in some remote parts of their brains, they refused to bring it to the forefront. And they certainly refused to acknowledge it in any tangible way. The door between their apartments remained open at all times, giving an al fresco feel to their living arrangement. If Lainey was cooking and ran out of an ingredient, she went into Dexter's half the house and took it, whether he was home or not. And when he was home, he was more often in her part of the house anyway, only going home at night to sleep in his bed. After a while even that small separation began to feel odd. But if they weren't ready to acknowledge their growing dependence on each other during the daylight, they certainly weren't ready to address their growing longing for each other in the nighttime.

I must be lonelier than I realized, they would admit, if the subject ever popped to mind. Both of them felt comfortable enough to admit that much was true; they had been lonely, Lainey especially. Ever since she quit work, she had been isolated from other people. For her Dexter clearly filled a void. Both of them could see and admit as much. But that was as far as Dexter was willing to go. If his brain started to probe any deeper, he would staunchly cut it off with a quick and ready rejoinder. *I like her; she's likeable. Of course I enjoy her company, look at the alternative.* That was an easy one to believe because, in comparison to The Russians, Lainey was clearly the preferable and more enjoyable choice. Plus she smelled good and she fed him. What wasn't to love? *Not that I love her,* he hastened to tell himself. In a friend way, perhaps. They were decidedly friends, the type who had fun, ate all their meals together, and spent all their evenings cuddling on the couch.

The cuddling was part of the contract, Dexter assured himself. His newfound enjoyment of it was not, but he didn't discuss that part of things, not even with himself.

As for Lainey, life was looking up, if she also didn't let herself look too closely. There was Dexter, an unexpected delight. Who knew the stodgy neighbor would turn out to be secretly funny and, after a bit of practice, a deft hugger? Not her, that was for certain. When she agreed to marry Dexter for the sake of his job, she had envisioned a few awkward run-ins during times they were unable to avoid each other. Instead they had somehow become inseparable.

Her job was looking up, too, if she also didn't allow herself to delve too deeply. In reality she walked a razor's edge of disaster, one failed job away from losing everything. But if she didn't dwell on how abysmal her future was, she could feel cheerful about the present. The enrober *had* worked to increase her productivity. She was able to take on more jobs, as many as she could find. Currently she had a big order, her biggest one to date—five hundred oversized chocolate ants for a woman who wanted them as a giveaway for *her* new business. The whole thing felt symbiotic to Lainey, girl power and all that. Women supporting women. Maybe she should put that on her website, if she ever got a website. For the moment she was still relying on word of mouth, a few flyers she'd posted around town, and her Facebook page.

She finished packaging her 500th ant and checked her phone. The woman, Cheryl, had said she would text the dropoff location and it hadn't come through yet.

Finished the last ant, Lainey sent her. The return text came almost immediately, but Lainey had to read it three times to make certain she understood.

Forget it.

What? Lainey tried, but there was no response. She tried to call. There was no answer. She texted again. *I have your ants. Need the dropoff info and final payment.*

I'm canceling the ants. My loan fell through. The business is a no-go.

Lainey stared at her phone. This could not be happening. She had spent days upon days making these ants, had bought a hundred pounds of covuerture Belgian milk chocolate. Even with Dexter's generous discount, the financial outlay had been immense, not to mention the time it took to make each ant because the woman wanted buttercream faces piped on each one to highlight her up-and-coming organic makeup business.

You still have to pay, Lainey typed. *I've already made them. I'll deliver them and you can decide what to do with them.*

You can deliver them but I ain't paying.

It took a special sort of person to go to the trouble of typing bad grammar. Even most people who spoke it out of a lazy habit texted the proper word. Something about it now felt like purposeful anger, vengeance perhaps. With a sinking feeling, Lainey checked her bank, the place where a week ago she placed the woman's deposit check. She may not be a business genius, but she knew not to buy hundreds of dollars worth of ingredients and materials without a deposit. Except now there was no deposit. The check had bounced; Lainey's account was overdrawn.

Seeing spots, she sank to a chair and bent over.

Ruin. Disaster. Repossession.

She dashed upright and stared at her enrober. Would The Hungarians come and take it?

It's already paid for, she reassured herself. It was the less-tangible things now hanging in the balance. Insurance, rent, food, gas. She would need all of them in the coming days, and now there was no money.

She bent over again, trying hard not to hyperventilate. When the fog of panic began to ebb, she realized there was nothing she could do. Even if she was inclined to, she couldn't track down the woman and make her pay because she had no idea where she worked. Her gaze settled on the five hundred ants. They stared back at her, their overly vivid faces a tangible reminder of her failure.

I can turn this around, she thought, pulling deep for any hints of her former optimism. There was no chance she could re-sell them to someone else, not with the odd juxtaposition of bug and beautiful makeup. (Really, that should have been her first clue the woman's inner wheel had stopped turning, but she'd jumped at the chance to make something so unique.) At the very least she could make someone's day brighter. With renewed determination and a forced smile, she hopped up and began gathering the ants into their protective plastic bin. She would take them to a homeless shelter. Maybe they would go to someone who hadn't had chocolate in way too long; maybe they would still find a way to make someone smile.

This day won't be a total waste, Lainey told herself, beginning to feel some of the cheer she was trying desperately to fake.

"This day was a total waste."

That was what Dexter was finally able to get out of Lainey. At first it was just the wailing. He found her once again lying prone on her living room floor, a sad starfish. He sat beside her and petted her head.

"What's the matter?" He wasn't unduly alarmed. Lainey was a small person of big emotion. It was more concerning when she didn't feel something deeply. A closed off and withdrawn Lainey was terrifying. Thankfully it was also rare.

She shifted from her position on the floor, pelting herself into his lap instead. And that was when she told him her day had been a waste.

"Why?" he asked.

"Ants…makeup…ruined…fail…homeless…"

Those were the only discernable words, muffled as they were against his leg and by her tears.

"The ants' makeup got ruined?" he asked. It was a sign of how far they'd come together that the sentence made perfect sense. Had the buttercream slid off? That had been a concern in the testing phase.

She shook her head furiously back and forth. Clutching his shirt in both hands, she peeled herself away and finally faced him. "No, she c-canceled."

"Canceled? What do you mean she canceled?"

"I mean she nixed the ants. She didn't want them. Apparently her business fell through. It's a common theme. Girl power." One fist pumped weakly in the air while her face resumed its position against his thigh. He peeled it away again, needing to understand.

"Lainey, what? She canceled the order? With no warning?"

Lainey nodded.

"Who does that?" he said, outraged on her behalf.

"People who order ants wearing makeup, apparently. But that's not the worst part."

"It's not?"

She shook her head.

"What's the worst part?" His hand smoothed over her hair, unsticking the stuck pieces from her wet cheeks.

"I tried to donate them to a homeless shelter and they refused them. It's against the law or something because they don't have labels, and the way she said it, like I should be ashamed for suggesting it. Insult to massive injury." She wailed again and resumed her post, face mashed firmly against his leg.

Dexter could well imagine how it had been. He knew the type, a small-time bureaucrat who got a contact high off wielding a tiny amount of power. "There are plenty of places you can donate them."

She withdrew her head from its resting place again, pausing her weeping to blink at him. "There are?"

"Yes. It can't be anyone that takes government funds because of all the rules, but there are tons of private places that don't go in for that sort of nonsense and will be glad to have them. In fact a few of them serve children who would love, absolutely *love* those silly ants."

"Really?" Lainey whispered, a genuine smile beginning to take the place of the tears as she imagined kids enjoying her ants.

"Yes. They'll be a smash," Dexter assured her.

She took a shuddery little breath. "Okay. Thank you." She rested her face against his leg, cheek first instead of nose first this time so she could still breathe and communicate.

"Was that it?" he asked, sensing there was more.

When she froze, his hunch was confirmed. "Well," she drawled. "Her deposit check bounced."

"What? So she's a criminal on top of being a rotten person?"

"Apparently," Lainey agreed. "The ants deserve so much better than her."

"Lainey," he said, taking a bracing breath. They never discussed finances. It was one of the many taboo topics between them on an ever-growing list.

"Hmm," she said, sleepy after all the emotion she'd expended.

"That had to have taken a wrecking ball to your finances," he noted.

She froze again. "Oh. It will be okay," she said in a tone that convinced neither of them.

"I'll give you some money."

"You already gave me some money. I bought a Hungarian enrober."

"I'll give you some more money," he said.

"You can't do that."

"Of course I can. Why not?"

"Because it wasn't in the contract and you said…"

He rolled his eyes. "I said I won't fix you, but this wasn't what I was talking about, obviously. And technically we're married."

Her eyes rounded with renewed panic. "Are you afraid I'm going to wreck your pristine credit? I truly am the Titanic of people." Her hands pressed to her temples.

"I am not afraid of any such thing. Marital status has nothing to do with credit scores, unless we take out a loan together."

Lainey dropped her hands and blinked at him. "That's probably the sort of thing I should have investigated before we were married."

"Probably," he agreed.

"I bet you did, huh."

"I did, but then that's me."

"It's okay," she assured him, now resting her head on his shoulder. "I'm a pretty bad bet."

"I disagree." He kissed the top of her head and reached for her hand, giving it a squeeze. Strange how something that used to be so foreign to him—affection—now came so easily and without thought. "Are you going to take the money? Say yes."

"Yes. Thank you." When it came down to it, she had no choice, and that was what she hated the most. How had she gotten herself in this position? She left her last job because she wanted to be independent and instead she had traded dependence on an employer to dependence on Dexter. Somehow that was worse, and she didn't understand why. Was it because she didn't want to be Dexter's liability? For her entire life, everyone had reached a point where she became too much. What if that happened with Dexter? *It can't,* Lainey told herself.

Because if there was one thing she knew for certain it was that she could no longer contemplate a future without him.

"It's going to be okay," Dexter reassured her, giving her hand a squeeze. "It's only a little setback. You're going to bounce back."

He was right. She would bounce back from this setback. But if Dexter lost faith in her and decided he was done, what then? Because she didn't think she would ever bounce back from that. It was that realization, more than any other, that left her pale and silent, quaking with nerves and dread and not the post-weeping exhaustion Dexter presumed.

CHAPTER 19

During those rare moments when Lainey had a break between projects, she liked to go to her favorite coffee shop and brood. Not that she allowed herself to brood about her real life—that was too painful to contemplate. Between her dreary financial situation, Dexter, her family's disinterest in her life, and what happened with Ian, there was too much real life controversy to choose from and it could easily tip her over the edge into despair. And because she was a sunny, optimistic person who liked to dwell on the bright side, she refused to ruminate on her own crummy problems. Instead she selected a fantasy from the catalog she kept in her mind, usually something so far fetched it had no basis in real life, or certainly not her real life. In fact it was quite possible she'd lifted the entire daydream from a *Lifetime* movie.

Whatever the case, she ordered a latte and stared pensively out the window, thinking about the evil babysitter who'd kidnapped her precious child while she'd been distracted by postpartum depression. Or maybe today she should be the child who had been kidnapped, now grown and realizing something was amiss. Or was today the day she pretended to be the kidnapper, not evil but with a tragic back-story. Maybe she genuinely believed the kidnapped child was hers originally, kidnapped at birth? It was a lot to think about and hash out and she was happy for the mental tidal wave that kept her from thinking about real life. Bonus points for the rain today, which helpfully added to her internal melodrama.

She was knees-deep in trying to figure out how to launder money to fund her new pretend life on the lam when the back door tinkled, causing her head to turn instinctively in that direction. It shouldn't have been a shock to see Ian enter—it was a mutually beloved coffee shop—but it still was. She hadn't seen him since that moment when she confessed her love and he scampered away in terror.

The terror was still in place today, comingling with horror when recognition hit. He froze, eyes wide, mouth ajar. But before he could sprint away, Lainey took control. Maybe it was because she had just been imagining making a quick getaway from the police or maybe it was because she still felt the potent sting of mortification. Whatever the reason she grabbed her keys and purse and jetted out the front door like her tail was on fire, not bothering to see what Ian might do, if he planned to do anything but spring out the door nearest him, which he undoubtedly intended before Lainey made her escape. Lainey had watched his hand reach for the handle and it had felt like a second rejection, so she made her split second decision and bounded away first.

But then she was stuck. She had come in through the back. In order to get to her car, she would have to circle around the entire shopping complex, in full view of the coffee shop and Ian. So instead she turned right and walked another familiar path, opening a door and stepping inside.

The coffee shop was providentially near Lainey's favorite candy store, one that had been in existence for as long as she could remember and probably a long time before that, run by an old man named Mr. Weaver who looked like Willy Wonka's understudy.

Now she paused in the entryway, comforted by the familiar scent of fresh chocolate, and stared at the vast displays.

They were different from her candies for certain, more old school —lots of dipped chocolates and creams. No sculptures, no ants wearing makeup (which had been such a hit at the preschool she donated them to that she decided to make them a regular part of her offerings.) But the shop had been there for as long as Lainey could remember, and it looked like the place that had been there even longer, probably since before she was born.

Why does everyone else succeed when I can only fail, she wondered.

"Good afternoon. See anything you like?"

The elderly owner, Mr. Weaver, toddled out from a back room and stood behind the counter staring at Lainey who couldn't seem to think of one word in reply.

He tipped his head. "Do you need more time, or can I help you?"

Finally Lainey was ready to reply. She opened her mouth, gulped a deep breath, and burst into loud, convulsive tears.

"It smells good in here," Dexter said when he let himself into Lainey's half of the house. He always expected it to smell good, and it never disappointed. He had come to associate pleasant smells with Lainey, so much that when a new peach supplier arrived at the office with a case of samples for them to try, he immediately pulled out his phone and sent her a text, a Pavlovian response to tantalizing scents.

"We're having pot roast," Lainey said.

She sat at the kitchen table, head down and resting on her arm. Dexter pinched a piece of chocolate from the bowl of odds and ends she'd started setting aside for him. He sat beside her.

"What's wrong?"

"Nothing."

"Lies." He poked her. "What's wrong?"

"I'm thinking of quitting my job," she blurted.

"I thought you already did that."

"That was my last job. I'm thinking of quitting this one."

"How do you do that? Give yourself two weeks notice?"

When she merely nodded in reply, he knew she was serious.

"Hey, what's going on? Talk to me."

"Nothing. This is me being reasonable. It's time to end this and get a real job again," she said. Dexter eyed her as she got up to remove the roast from the oven, giving it a poke before putting it back in again.

"I don't like this," he said. She was missing all her Lainey sparkle. He hated to see her so defeated. On the other hand, what if it was for the best? She'd tried an experiment and it failed. It happened to people every day. Maybe she should return to work before she got too far underwater, incurred debt it could take decades to undo.

"Neither do I," she sighed, resuming her seat. "When I was a kid, my dad always had big dreams. He quit more jobs than I could count, was always looking for the next big thing."

"Does realizing you're like him upset you?" he asked.

Her jaw dropped and she made a little gasping sound like he'd stabbed her. Before he could begin to even realize he'd upset her, she turned and fled up to her bedroom, slamming the door. Dexter remained frozen, flabbergasted and annoyed. Of *course* she was the kind of person who ran off to her bedroom in a heap of emotion in the middle of an otherwise rational discussion. The question now was which sort of man was he? The kind who went after her, or the kind who returned to the safety of his own home?

His glance slid longingly toward the door and freedom. Then, with a sigh, he headed toward her room. Would she lock the door? No. He wondered if that was a sign she secretly wanted him to follow.

He didn't bother to knock because who else would it be but him? He opened the door and let his senses acclimate to her room. It looked about like he remembered—not a sty, but not immaculate. Sort of organized chaos, much like Lainey. She didn't stir when he opened the door, meaning he had to go farther in to get a reaction. He took a few steps in and cleared his throat.

She remained hunched in a tiny ball like a wounded pill bug.

"Psst," he tried.

No reaction.

His gaze slid warily to the bed. Dare he lay in bed next to his wife? It seemed he would have to because he'd reached the going for broke point. He picked up a pair of leggings and set them aside, followed by a bra he touched with only the tips of his fingers. He flung it away and wiped his hand on his pants before he could absorb any girl cooties or wasteful emotions.

The bed sunk low beneath him, forming around him as if it remembered the shape of his dent. *I have a dent in Lainey's bed.* He pushed the thought aside as he lay down beside her and eased closer.

She continued to ignore him.

Even though common sense told him not to touch her when she was so closed off, some instinct made him reach out and smooth his hand gently along her arm and—miraculously—she softened a bit and unfurled, like a touch-me-not in reverse. "Lainey."

"What?" Her tremulous little whisper did something to him, something uncomfortably akin to queasiness. He didn't like that quaver, and he liked even less that he'd been the one to put it there. Or had he?

"Did I upset you?"

She rolled onto her back and glared up at him with tear filled eyes. "Seriously?"

Once again his hand reached out, this time stroking the side of her wet face. "I'm not so good at peopleing. You know this about me. I need you to tell me things. Don't assume I know them."

The lip wobble became more pronounced and tears leaked out her eyes at a faster rate. "You hurt my feelings."

The queasy feeling in his gut intensified. "I did? How?"

"You think I'm a dreamer, doomed to fail."

"What? How did you get that from what I said?" he asked, thoroughly confused as he reviewed the conversation in his head. In his mind, he'd merely been stating facts. She had, in fact, quit her job to follow her dream, like her father who had also done the same.

"You think I'm like my dad," she exclaimed.

"Well, kind of, you are," he said, glad they were back on the same page, at least until she wailed in misery. Except this time she didn't pull away from him; this time she went full barrel into him, pressing her face to his chest and clutching his shirt in her hand where it lay at his stomach. For a minute, he held her and let her cry and it was odd how much he didn't mind. Formerly Dexter hadn't been comfortable with any excess shows of emotion, and yet he'd held Lainey while she wept so many times he'd lost count. And he didn't hate it at all. In fact it gave him a strange feeling of purpose and power in the pit of his gut. Lainey cried and he could make her feel better, could make her soften up and stop crying. That yield was kind of amazing, like cuddling a sleeping puppy. After a while her sobs died down to sniffles. Exhausted, she lay curled in his embrace, still clutching his shirt.

"I don't want to be like him, Dexter," she said at last.

"Why not, Lainey?"

"Because his dreams always came first. Before me and Murphy, before our mom, before our finances, our house. It was always about his dreams and what made him feel good, what made him feel fulfilled. And it wasn't that his dreams always failed, it was that he always failed to put us first. Sometimes you have to take the loss in order to be a team player, unless you're my dad, then it's always about finding a personal win."

Dexter's hand continued to smooth gently up and down her arm as he let her words sink in, trying to understand them. "So even though you and your dad have that thing in common, even though you both left a job to pursue a dream, you see yourself as different because you're willing to take the loss. You're not willing to make others suffer for your own selfish ambition."

"Yes, although…" she swallowed hard and made herself say it. "The only person I have to make suffer is you and I…" *Say it, Lainey. Admit the hard truth.* "I want you to be proud of me. I don't want to fail in your eyes."

His hand paused its journey up and down her arm. "I see. Did you already take another job?"

"I talked to a guy, Mr. Weaver. He runs that candy shop in the little complex out on the highway. When I told him how much I loved candy, he suggested I work for him. It's not enough to fix all my financial woes, but it's a start. Enough to give me some breathing room. Maybe…maybe I'll be able to keep taking some orders on the side."

They both knew she wouldn't, though. The nature of her work was immersive, requiring hours upon hours of intense labor. There was no time to do it and hold another job, especially when she could barely get everything done as it was.

"Why don't you think about it a couple of weeks, okay? Maybe something will turn around in the meantime. Don't make any decisions until after the party and then…"

They both froze, sudden tension and awareness bouncing between them. And then what? What would happen after the party? What would happen to Lainey's job? What would happen to *them*? Would they jointly discover some magic to fix everything they pretended not to notice?

"And then we'll circle back around and figure out a solution, okay?" Dexter said.

"Okay," Lainey said, happy for a reprieve. She wanted it both ways, she realized. She wanted the safety and security of a nine to five job with the adventure and promise of following her dream. But that rarely worked out. No one could have everything, it was always either/or. Dexter had chosen safety and security, and he was doing okay. Did that mean she should, too?

And then there was Dexter himself. He was the nine to five version of a relationship—solid, secure, dependable. But was he also the adventure? Was he the dream? Or would that forever be reserved for Ian, who had been her ideal for so long?

Not that it mattered. She was married to Dexter, if only technically, and Ian was so far gone after her flopped pronouncement that he'd left permanent dust trails in his wake.

"You're so tense," Dexter noted. He pulled her closer, curving her back against his front.

"Look at you, you're a pro snuggler now," Lainey said, nestling.

"The big snuggling leagues keep trying to recruit me, but I'm keeping my options open," he said.

"Steer clear of the Ivy League," she warned. "They're all for show, lots of cuddling bling, not a lot of cuddling substance."

"I'm leaning toward the Big Ten."

She giggled a little Lainey laugh. "What's the Big Ten?"

"Golden retrievers, kittens, bunnies, babies, otters, piglets, calves, cockatoos, sugar gliders, and…" He needed a tenth. What was the cuddliest thing he could think of? "And Lainey." He gave her a squeeze.

"Go Team Lainey," she said, weaving her fingers through his.

"Go Team Lainey," he agreed, giving her a full body squeeze.

She rolled onto her back, facing him. "You're pretty good at the fake husbanding stuff."

"You should see what I can do with the real kind," he said, sliding his leg over hers.

She let out a puff of laughter that was half surprise, half nerves. They didn't ever go there, to the real side. They kept things light and neutral and if either of them had other ideas, they kept them safe inside. She knew he was only joking, but it still shocked her to hear it. "Wowzers," she drawled.

He tugged her slightly closer and wagged his brows.

"I can't tell if you're joking," she said softly.

"Neither can I," he said equally as softly. His finger stroked under her chin, angling her face toward his.

She sucked in a little breath. "Wh…what are we doing here?"

"I don't know. I think maybe your tears short-circuited my brain, but who cares? Now would be a perfect time to stop thinking," Dexter returned.

"If you're the one saying that, this ship has already run aground," she said.

"Probably, but at this particular moment, maybe I don't care."

"It's the maybe that gives me pause. We…we have a contract." She swallowed hard.

"It was never notarized," he said, brushing his nose on hers.

Lainey felt like she was having an out-of-body experience. This was *Dexter*. He was supposed to be the easygoing one, the laidback softie who got her over this rough patch. And yet here he was, apparently making a move. It was hard not to contrast him with Ian, whose panic had been so intense it had radiated off him like an aura. She had always thought Ian was brave because he ran into burning buildings, but perhaps there were other kinds of bravery. Maybe making the first move was its own kind of bravery. The question was what to do about it. What should she say? Something smooth and diplomatic.

"My bell is ringing."

His lashes fluttered. "What?"

"The timer. Downstairs. Pot roast?" Why did she make pot roast sound like a question? It was definitively pot roast.

"Yes, your bell," he said, tucking a wayward hair behind her ear. Then he swept her into his embrace and rolled to the opposite side, depositing her deftly on her feet in one swift movement.

"Were you in the circus? That was some kind of acrobat maneuver," she said. She told herself that was why she felt so disoriented.

In answer, he gave her another one of those suggestive eyebrow wags that set her heart aflutter.

"Pot roast?" she said, cheeks flushing.

"You tell me," he said.

She hesitated, but the timer would not be denied and either she was too practical to risk charred roast or she was too cowardly to stay and face whatever happened next. In any case she spun and fled down the stairs.

CHAPTER 20

For a few days, the new life they'd established continued unabated, and neither mentioned the strange interlude in Lainey's bedroom. The Russians were still deep in party planning. Dexter didn't tell Lainey how many grandiose plans he had to tamp down on a daily basis, more because he was afraid she'd be disappointed when there was no live chainsaw ice sculpture carving or caviar and blini buffet. Sometimes he wondered if The Russians were as insane as they made themselves out to be or if they enjoyed testing him. Then he remembered that when he first joined the company he cleaned out a drawer and found a list titled, "Hitmen Who Will Work For Rubles" and thought it was always better to err on the side of safety.

As elaborate as their plans sometimes were, they proved a safe distraction from the looming threat of The Hungarians. In their latest endeavor to gain The Popovs' attention, they had taken out an aggressive billboard that featured four babies in strollers, their faces swapped out for those of the four Popov brothers. It was a safe bet no one outside the industry noticed or cared about the rivalry, but to The Russians it was everything. Dexter wasn't certain how much longer he could hold back the surging tide of their hostility. And, if he were being honest, The Hungarians annoyed him, too. Why did they have to pop onto the scene now, when they had just added The Bristol account and needed every appearance of civility and class?

Those had become the big buzzwords around the office, along with high road and *men.* Dexter's tactic was to try and convince the brothers that real men did the right thing and set their sights higher than petty rivalries. For the moment it was working, but sometimes he felt like he was the second to last drip of water before the tide breached the floodgate. Needless to say there was a lot of tension in the air, which the upcoming party helped to diffuse, at least at work. At home it was another matter.

The problem was that neither Lainey nor Dexter had found the courage to address what would happen after the party. In the beginning it had seemed far off. They'd have a few months, multiple weeks to play at being married, and then it would be over. What neither counted on was how very much they would enjoy their imaginary relationship, nor how hard it would be to see it end. And so, as with everything, they kept on pretending. The party would be fine. They'd deal with everything later. Certainly they'd find a resolution that suited them both, one that didn't require either of them to search their hearts or make a declaration.

Magic. They were both relying on magic.

At the current moment, Lainey was also relying on work magic, but her rainbow-laced world was starting to fray and crumble. Even after the timely cash infusion from Dexter, things were starting to unravel. There was only so much shifting she could do, only so much sleight of hand before things started to reveal themselves. She was working as hard as she could, taking as many jobs as she could handle, pushing herself beyond every limit. And it wasn't enough. She couldn't make enough to cover rent, utilities, insurance, her car, gas, and food.

Fail, fail, fail, fail, fail. The refrain ran through her mind at all times of the day and night. It woke her from a deep sleep, pounding relentlessly like a drum. The only time it was ever on mute was when she was with Dexter. Then it played softly in the background, along with, *What will he think of you when he finds out?*

That, at least, she could put to rest. Dexter didn't care about her job. In fact he would probably feel better when she gave up her dream and returned to being a cog, like him. It was much more secure that way, and Dexter liked security.

And yet somehow in a way she didn't understand, even that thought hurt her, the one that said Dexter would like her better if she had a real job. It wouldn't be so bad to work for Mr. Weaver, but was it a step backwards instead of forward? Was it an admission of defeat and failure? If not, why did it feel that way? She swore she would never end up like her dad, would never pursue a fanciful pipe dream at the cost of everything real. But how was what she was doing now any different? It had felt different, when she quit her job. She'd had a plan; she'd had orders lined up. But the reality didn't pan out the way she'd thought. She vastly underestimated how much work it would take to start a business and stay financially afloat. Really, she vastly overestimated herself. Once again and in a different way, she wasn't enough.

Fail, fail, fail, fail. The words filtered through her mind. She pushed them away, trying to put on a happy face. A quick glance at the clock told her it was almost time for Dexter to come home.

⚷

*L*ainey was sad, or maybe worried. Dexter could tell by the expression on her face. It was the same one she'd been wearing since she mentioned working for Mr. Weaver, and though he should probably be relieved she had an out from her current situation, along with a plan for her future, in reality he felt sad. Dexter wasn't the type of person who had big dreams. He was happy with the status quo, happy to work a safe job and lead a safe life. But Lainey was the kind of woman who needed her dreams, and for that reason all of them should come true.

"Hey," he said, resting his shoulder in the doorway of her kitchen.

She glanced up at him with a smile that became more genuine, so deep it made her dimple pop. "Robert."

"It's Dexter," he said.

"Where?"

"You're definitively insane."

She laughed and used her elbow to push the hair out of her face. As usual, she was working. She worked constantly, was trying so hard to make it. It broke something in Dexter that she wasn't succeeding.

"Chocolate fingers," he noted.

"Completely impaired," she agreed, sounding tired. Guessing by the amount of chocolate layers on her fingers, she'd been working a while, had been on her feet in the same position for hours, maybe since he went to work that morning. She had to be exhausted, and yet she kept going. It wasn't fair to try so hard and still not win. Something in his chest prodded painfully, urging his feet forward.

"How can I help?" he asked.

"I'm almost done actually, but thanks," she said, eyes and attention dropping to her work.

Dexter had no idea why his feet kept walking toward her, only that they seemed unable to stop. And when he was close enough he stood behind her and rested his hands on her hips, using his thumbs to massage her lower back. She paused and melted against him a little.

"How did you know that's where it hurts?" she asked.

"Lucky guess," he said, leaning forward to press his lips to that spot where spine met skull, conveniently exposed by her wayward messy bun. He had no idea he was going to kiss her until he did it, but when she gasped and tilted her head, allowing him better access, he knew it was the right thing, the natural thing. Of *course* he should kiss his wife. Why wouldn't he?

"Oh, that's...okay, yes then 'cause...words hard now..." Lainey murmured.

"How close to done is 'close'?" Dexter asked, lips migrating to the side of her neck.

"Done...'cause..."

"Words?" he guessed, switching to the other side.

"Yep."

"Good. Let's get you cleaned up." He ushered her to the sink and turned it on, sticking his finger under the tap to check the temperature. When it was properly warm, he tugged her hands under the spray and began washing them for her, removing the layers of chocolate.

"This is nice," Lainey said, standing still while he soaped and rinsed her. "The caring."

"You work so hard, Lainey. So hard."

"'S okay," she said, suddenly choked.

"Let's take the night off and do something special," he suggested.

"Like what?" she asked.

"We'll go out to eat," he began.

"With you so far," she agreed.

"And then…"

"And then?"

Their eyes met and lingered, hands still joined and soapy. "And then let's see where it goes," he said.

"Are you hitting on me?" she asked.

"Well, you are my wife. Probably about time I got around to it," he said.

"Maybe a little past time," she said.

"Really," he drawled, pressing a kiss to her palm.

"So…" she began with no idea how to finish, but at that moment someone rang the doorbell.

Their eyes swiveled in that direction. "Are we expecting someone?" he asked.

"Everyone we know is here," she said. "Maybe a package?"

"We'd better beat the box people," he said. "I'll get it. You keep working on this. There's chocolate in unexpected places."

"You have no idea," she said, smiling when he laughed as he walked away.

Dexter opened the door, expecting to sign for a package, and encountered two men instead. One looked vaguely familiar, though Dexter was certain he'd never met him before. Right away the sight of them set off prickles of alarm. Were they grifters? Lainey was that type, easy prey for people with bad intent. She was much too soft-hearted and prone to fall for a sob story. His hand gripped the doorpost tighter.

"Is Lainey here?" the man closest to him asked. Again, Dexter didn't care for his tone, a combination of proprietary and condescending.

"Who's asking?" Dexter replied.

The guy laughed, an unpleasant bark that said he was less than amused by Dexter's question, despite the fact that he was the one on the wrong side of the door. "Who's asking," he repeated, facing his companion. They were both beefy and built and Dexter began to wonder if they had something more nefarious than grifting in mind.

"And who are you?" the first man asked, tone now decidedly belligerent.

"I'm her husband," Dexter replied and he could practically see the mental bomb land and detonate in front of them as their eyes widened with disbelief.

"What? No," the first man said while the second man said, "What?" twice.

"Would you like me to give her a message?" Dexter offered, now fully alarmed. Who were these people?

"Yes," the first man said. "Tell her that her brother would like a word."

CHAPTER 21

"Meep!"

The tiny squeak from behind Dexter alerted them to the fact that Lainey was there and had heard her brother's pronouncement. The three men turned to face her in unison, and she took a step back.

"Lainey," Murphy said in that way only brothers can, with full accusation and shaming.

Dexter, unable to stand the stark panic in her expression, held out his hand to her, inviting her to take a step closer and reach out. She did so, letting out a breath as she tucked her hand firmly in his.

"This guy says he's your husband," Murphy added. Now his tone demanded Lainey tell him it was all a big joke.

"Well, the thing is, um, he, um, is," Lainey said, purposely not looking at Ian. She didn't have to look to hear the sound he'd just made, as if all the air was suddenly sucked from his body.

"What the…" Murphy began, but Dexter interrupted. Belatedly he realized he was hovering protectively and that protectiveness wasn't helping diffuse the tense situation. He stepped aside.

"Maybe you should come in," he invited.

"Oh, gee, thanks for the invite, total stranger," Murphy said, full sarcasm.

"Murphy, please," Lainey said.

"Please what, Lainey? You are *married* and you didn't tell your family? Did you know?" He faced Ian who shook his head still looking dazed. He tried to catch Lainey's eyes, but she was still successfully dodging him.

"Does anyone want candy? I could arrange a plate." Lainey's gaze traveled helplessly toward the kitchen.

"Candy will not solve this," Murphy declared.

"Candy solves everything," Dexter said, giving Lainey's hand an encouraging squeeze. He could practically feel the blood draining from it, from her, and it set his already heightened emotions to "percolate." But he needed to be careful, to make a good impression on the brother she adored. Or rather try to salvage the poor impression he'd already made. Currently the two men were looking at him like *he* was the suspicious grifter, as if he wasn't the one who had been here every single day the last few weeks, watching Lainey struggle alone. If they were so vested, where had they been? And who was the other guy, the silent one whose gobsmacked expression looked like he'd been bashed in the face by a large frying pan?

Lainey laughed weakly and shot Dexter a helpless plea. What did she want from him in this situation? To play the husband or explain the truth? For that matter, what was the truth? Every day the water became a bit muddier.

Murphy and the other guy, whose name Dexter would soon learn was Ian, came in and closed the door. And then Murphy faced his sister, arms crossed. "You have some explaining to do."

"Well," Lainey began, shooting Dexter another of those looks so that even though he told himself not to interfere, he felt himself take a breath to do exactly that.

"Did we know you were coming?" Dexter blurted.

Murphy and Ian scowled at him. "What?" Murphy said.

"Did Lainey know you were coming? You live in Florida, right? Seems far away for a drop by visit."

"Oh, so you do know about me," Murphy said.

"Of course I do. Lainey talks about you a lot. I think maybe you're her favorite person," Dexter said, tossing Lainey a smile. "Which makes it all the odder that we had no idea you were coming."

"I decided to surprise her," Murphy said.

"Surprise," Lainey said weakly, waving her free arm in what might have been a failed attempt at jazz hands, a thing she did when she felt nervous or awkward.

"It's just that if she knew you were coming, I'm sure she would have tried to prepare you for this," Dexter said, raising his hand where it was joined to Lainey's.

Lainey nodded her frantic agreement. "Yes. I would have...tried... to...explain and prepare. Are we sure no one wants candy?" Her eyes shot hopefully to the kitchen again. Dexter wasn't certain if she truly believed candy would redeem the situation or if she was merely desperate for escape. Perhaps she was planning to shimmy out the tiny window over the kitchen sink.

"Try now," Murphy demanded. "I'm listening."

Lainey took a breath. "Well, Dexter was my neighbor." She pointed behind them to Dexter's shared wall. "And we both had these...there was a jar of cherries...I needed...The Russians...The Party...and now there are Hungarians. You know?"

Far from looking befuddled, Murphy and Ian stared at her as if this was par for the course with Lainey. Of course she would offer a baffling explanation of an even more baffling event. Dexter did not like that look, not one bit, because how dare they find Lainey anything but an adorable delight? Yes, she spoke in riddles, but in the best possible way and from an overflowing heart. So once again Dexter found himself about to provide a reprieve.

"It was one of those things," Dexter said. "Kismet." He brought their still joined hands to his lips and kissed Lainey's knuckles and she blushed, playing her part well. Or maybe she wasn't playing anymore. Who knew? Not him.

"You married a stranger and didn't tell us," Murphy said slowly, angrily.

Lainey let go of Dexter's hand to toss up both her hands in frustration. "When would I have told you, Murphy? When you were dodging my calls? Not returning them? Letting them go to voicemail? Did you want me to leave you a message? *Hi, it's your sister. I met the best guy, and I'm marrying him because no one else wants me.*" Her voice broke.

"Lainey," Ian finally spoke, his first word since the initial "what." He reached out a beseeching hand. Lainey pivoted away from him and swiped her eyes, taking a shaky breath.

Dexter remained in the center of it, calculating how best to diffuse the tension. This was what he did, and he was pretty good at it, if he did say so. He took a breath and aimed for a friendly tone, one that wasn't much of a reach, "Have you guys eaten? Because Lainey and I are starved, and we were about to get food. Why don't I order some barbecue and we can sit down and talk."

Ian still looked tense and miserable and—guilty? What was that about? But Murphy softened his stance, if only a little.

"I could go for some food," he murmured.

"Good," Dexter said with a nod. "Lainey and I found a good place, a hole in the wall, and they deliver. I'll call it in and then for dessert we could, I don't know, eat chocolate perhaps. My wife makes a stellar makeup ant."

Lainey snorted a little laugh, as he knew she would. It was wobbly, but it would get better, he'd see to it. He gave her shoulder a squeeze. She tossed him a warm smile in return, and he reached for his phone.

❦

As the night wore on, Murphy became less suspicious, more relaxed, more willing to give Dexter a chance. And Dexter was killing it, if he did say so himself, at least with Murphy. Murphy was impressed by his job and his manner, probably thinking the calmness made a good foil for Lainey's high passion. Dexter thought so, too, an unforeseen and happy circumstance of their sham marriage. They actually were good together, exceptional, really, and he vowed to circle back and think about that fact later. But not now, not when there was still so much to be done to smooth the rough and awkward night.

In the end most of the awkwardness had stemmed from Ian, and Dexter didn't understand. Was he that protective of his best friend's little sister? Did he believe Murphy was being blinded by Dexter? Or was it something else? Did Ian have a crush on Lainey? Had he believed he would end up with her and saw Dexter as a rival?

He put that away to think about later, too.

The food arrived. It smelled good and tasted delicious and for a while they ate, Lainey and Murphy making pleasant small talk about their family. Murphy and his dad were hard at work on their latest venture, an alligator farm, and Dexter had a lot of questions about that. Ian was a local firefighter, but his stoic expression and angry silence didn't invite questions, so Dexter asked him none.

By the end of the evening, everyone but Ian had mellowed considerably. Dexter liked Murphy and thought he loved Lainey as much as she loved him. But they were different, vastly so. Murphy was more reserved with his affection, emotions, and words. He wasn't a phone guy; he was a show up in person and demand answers guy. Now that he'd received them, he seemed satisfied. And Lainey seemed happy that her brother had an actual interest in her life.

The evening began to wind down to a natural close. *We did it,* Dexter congratulated himself. They had successfully convinced Lainey's brother and friend that they were a happily married couple. Then, as always, he realized he was premature in his self-congratulatory conceit when Murphy stood, stretched, yawned, and spoke.

"Is it okay if I stay here?"

"Yes," Lainey gushed, full enthusiasm as always. "You're always welcome here, you know that."

"I knew it when you were single, not so sure about now," Murphy said. His eyes traveled questioningly to Dexter. Lainey's eyes traveled to him in panic as realization hit: if Murphy stayed, they'd have to continue the charade that their marriage was real, that Dexter didn't go to his own apartment at the end of the night.

"Absolutely," Dexter said. "Always welcome." He gave Lainey's back a little pat, trying to push the panic out of her eyes. It would be fine. They'd been married for weeks. Surely they could safely cohabitate for one night. Couldn't they?

CHAPTER 22

While Murphy showered, Dexter sneaked to his apartment to grab his things—toiletries for tonight and clothes for work in the morning. He had no idea what Lainey did during that time, but when he arrived in her bedroom she was tucked in, hands clutching the blanket to her chin.

"You look like a virgin bride I just bought off the internet," Dexter said.

"That's maybe how I feel," Lainey agreed, blinking up at him with big eyes.

"Relax. I'm not going to ravish you." He paused. "Unless you want me to?"

She bit her lip and let go of her tight grip on the covers. "Let's start with talking and see how it goes."

"Excellent. This is no big deal, you know. Lots of guys have sleepovers with their wives. I've always wanted to. This is a bucket list thing. Don't ruin it for me."

She snorted a laugh and relaxed further, pushing down the covers a bit to reveal her sleep attire—an oversized t-shirt with a picture of Albert Einstein.

"Somehow I knew when this moment came I would share it with a German scientist," Dexter said.

She giggled again and the last of the tension drained out of her. "Thanks for being so great about tonight. About everything, really."

"You're welcome, but I didn't do anything. You shouldn't thank someone for common decency and good manners."

"But they're rare," Lainey said.

Knowing what Dexter knew of the world, he couldn't disagree. He started to undress and realized she was watching him. "You're staring. People don't usually stare when I do this."

"Would it make you feel less objectified if I tossed some dollar bills at you and hummed a sultry little tune?" she asked.

"Whatever floats your boat, although I have to say it's a little unfair that you're getting the Full Monty here and I missed the show entirely." He shucked out of his pants and shirt, folded them neatly, and laid them on the chair at the edge of the room, one that was currently draped with no less than five of her shirts and leggings.

"I don't think this is the Full Monty," she said, regarding his t-shirt and boxers.

"It's the principle of the thing," he declared, arranging his loafers so they were properly aligned at a ninety degree angle under her chair.

"In my defense it took me thirty seconds to toss my clothes into a basket and put on this shirt and you're taking so long I'm beginning to wonder if you're gunning for a clothes arranging management position," she said. "Why do you keep moving the shoes? They're not going to walk away. They'll still be in the same position in the morning."

"I can't sleep if the angle isn't right," he said.

"What about all of my stuff? Doesn't it bother you that it's haphazardly strewn?" she said.

"I don't see it. I think my brain has put up some kind of protective veil that doesn't allow me to process your mess or else I would spend all my time arranging everything." He waved a hand in front of his face.

"You're all kinds of fun," she said.

He laughed and tossed himself onto the bed beside her. "Says the woman who actually uttered the word 'meep' when her brother arrived."

"Don't disparage 'meep.' It's the thing you say when the emotions are too big and nothing else will do."

"You're pretty cute, for a crazy person," he said, pushing the stray hairs off her face. She had taken down the messy bun and now her hair was curly. He thought it was beyond cute; it was adorable. This was Lainey at her essence, soft and warm and undone.

"You're not so bad yourself. A little overdressed, though." She tapped his t-shirt. "I didn't know people still wore these white Underoos. Tell me, do your garters hold your socks up well, or do they occasionally slip?"

With a heavy sigh, he sat up and took off his shirt. He started to fold it, but she snatched it away and tossed it onto the Chair Of Things.

"That's going to wrinkle," he said, tone pained.

"So am I, if you wait any longer to come to bed," she said. "Why are you still on top of the covers? Are you afraid of me? Are my wiles more potent than I know?"

He surveyed her, streaky blond hair splayed alluringly on her pillow, folded softly as if someone had carefully laid her out for his inspection. Was she still wearing makeup, or was she actually that pretty in the middle of bedtime?

"Meep," he said and was rewarded when she laughed. She held the covers up for him and he slipped beneath them, somehow managing to reach for her in the process. She snuggled into him with a little sigh of contentment. He kissed the top of her head.

Since he had taken off his shirt, her sleepy fist had nothing to twine. She contented herself with stretching her fingers over his stomach, brushing her thumb over the hairs there. He could feel her slipping toward slumber, but he was anything but sleepy. As the moments ticked, he became more awake, more aware. It was as if every stroke of her thumb on his stomach shot little pinpricks of electricity to all the other parts of him, telling him to wake up, step up, be a man, and do something important.

He shifted toward her slightly and let his hand glide from its resting spot at her waist to grip behind her thigh, tugging her insistently closer. Her eyes popped open.

"Oh, hey, you're still here," she murmured.

"Yep," he said.

"Hmm."

They stared at each other. He could see the uncertainty and indecision warring in her features and he let her stew, not wanting to push her in any direction. If they took an irredeemable step, he wanted it to be fully her decision with no coercion from him. That meant he had to be hands off, quite literally, because he was definitely in the mood to coerce.

He remained painfully frozen for what felt like an eternity, allowing her to think it through and decide. When she finally tipped forward and brushed her lips on his, he wanted to throw an impromptu ticker-tape parade. Instead he settled for kissing her back, molding her body against his while his lips worked her to remain soft and yielding. Even in his love-drunk haze, he understood hard and insistent kisses were not the way right now. Lainey was vulnerable.

She made a sweet little sound—of pleasure or surrender? He had no idea, but it nearly drove him over the edge of reason as she twined her arms around him and plunged her fingers in his hair, deepening the kiss. He was almost too far gone, almost under completely, but one tiny thought kept trying to intrude, dragging him back to reality.

Lainey was vulnerable. Why was Lainey vulnerable? What was he trying so hard to simultaneously remember and also forget? What happened to Lainey that made her vulnerable to his words, his kisses, his affection and attention?

The little voice grew louder and more insistent as little snippets of memory began to filter back to him. At last that voice became louder than all the others and he broke away, putting a few inches between them as he sucked oxygen.

"Meep?" Lainey tried.

He shook his head and held up a hand. What was he doing? This was everything he wanted. Was he the biggest idiot in the world? Undoubtedly yes, but he couldn't stop his lips from uttering what came next.

"Lainey, who is Ian?"

"*D*exter is sad," Yuri declared. Once again the brothers had been staring at him all morning.

"Dexter is fine," Dexter assured them. Their office had multiple spaces for multiple uses, and yet somehow the five of them always ended up in the conference room together with Dexter as the honorary little brother, privy to all their teasing and jabs.

"No, is droopy face. Look at it. Mr. Floppy Jowls," Maxim added.

"No floppy jowls. Just Dexter."

"Is trouble in married paradise," Andrei guessed.

"No trouble, just a short night," Dexter said and regretted giving them even that much when they wolf whistled and high fived his good fortune. "Not like that. I didn't sleep well, that's all."

"You always sleep well," Ivan accused, squinting. "Why no sleep now? Is business bad?"

"Is bankruptcy, yes?" Yuri said, leaning forward in sudden anxiety.

"I will go dismantle marble from entrance," Andrei volunteered.

"Stop, no, come back," Dexter called because already Andrei was halfway out the door and heading for the emergency crowbar. It was good to know the brothers kept it to dismantle the marble and not to beat their enemies, especially with the threat of The Hungarians still looming.

He took a breath. "Business is fine, amazing, in fact. We've never been better. Even The Bristols are happy." He almost beamed, but he couldn't help it. The brothers had been doing an amazing job of keeping their noses clean lately, which was especially miraculous with The Hungarians always hovering on the periphery, trying to provoke a response.

"Then why Mr. Floppy Jowls?" Ivan asked.

"I'm not…I don't have…" Dexter said, massaging the pressure point between his eyes.

"Is Lainey? Is crazy?"

"Of course not. I mean sort of, but in a good way," Dexter said. There was no way he could tell the brothers what was actually going on, no way he could seek their advice. Could he?

When he dropped his hand, they were all staring at him, matching expressions of dark concern.

"I met her brother," he said.

"And he is crazy," Maxim guessed. "You maybe need us to make him disappear?"

"What? No, don't disappear anyone. He's fine. He lives in Florida. I probably won't see him very much."

"Then what is problem? He is not approving of you for sister?"

"He seemed to approve okay. But he has this best friend, Ian."

"Grown man with best friend? Are you sure he's grown?" Andrei said.

"Is American," Maxim reminded them, and they nodded their combined understanding.

"Brother has bestie. Continue," Ivan invited.

"The guy, the best friend, he's sort of…he was kind of…I think Lainey's in love with him."

The brothers stared at him, silent and unblinking until at last Maxim mustered a response. "And he's the one you want us to make disappear? The one your wife is cheating with?"

"Would not be the first time," Yuri said, and the other brothers again nodded their agreement.

"No, it's not like that. She's not cheating. She hasn't spoken to him since we got married. And she told me up front about him, but back then it was all theoretical, and now…"

"Is real," Yuri guessed.

Dexter nodded.

"This is why Popovs do not fall in love. Destroys a man from the inside," Ivan said, dabbing the heel of his palm against his eyes as Yuri gave an oversized sniff.

"If we are not making man disappear, what are we to do?" Andrei asked.

"Nothing," Dexter said. "I knew going into it what the deal was. I can only be who I am. Everything else is on Lainey."

"No, I refuse to accept," Maxim said, banging his fist on the table.

"Is time for grand gesture," Yuri declared.

"Yes, grand gesture," Andrei agreed. The other brothers nodded their enthusiastic agreement, too.

"I don't do grand gestures," Dexter reminded them. "That's not me. I'm a slow-and-steady-wins-the-race kind of guy."

"But in real life slow and steady guy gets run over by guy in tank," Ivan said.

"Happened to our Uncle Lev," Yuri said, crossing himself. "Rest his soul."

"There's nothing I can do," Dexter said. "It's up to Lainey now. The party is in two weeks, and then she'll need to decide how this thing ends."

"Dexter, don't take wrong way, okay? Is not insult, is observation: you are too passive, like little girl. Women, they don't like that. Women like men, real men who act like men. Who make big declaration with grand gesture."

"Let us help with gesture, yes?" Ivan said hopefully as the other brothers leaned forward.

"Guys, don't take this the wrong way, okay? It's not an insult, it's an observation: absolutely none of you has ever had a successful relationship, let alone been married."

"Oh, so harsh, Dexter," Ivan said, dabbing his eyes again.

Dexter sighed. "This is not an appropriate work topic, and I would love to drop it. Can we please get back to work?"

"Yes, but you are making big mistake," Yuri said.

"Big mistake," the other brothers echoed before, thankfully, returning their attention to work.

Their productivity was short lived when Sonya arrived, taking a seat at the table without a word until she had every man's rapt attention. One by one they stopped what they were doing and stared at her, waiting for her to speak. Dexter was the last to give in and focus on her, and he was apparently the one she was waiting for because she remained mute until she had his full notice.

"The Hungarians are on the move," she declared.

"The move? What do you mean the move?" Dexter asked.

"They are gunning for The Bristols," Sonya said.

"How could you possibly know that?" Dexter asked.

"I know all," Sonya said. "I know, for instance, that is not love match with little American wife girl. Is, how you say, marriage of convenience?"

"That's not relevant to The Hungarians," Dexter said, waving her away.

"Is relevant to me, though, because after party, after sham marriage is over, you and I have some things to discuss, yes?"

With effort, Dexter controlled his shudder. He hadn't missed Sonya's attempts to pin him down—sometimes quite literally—these last few weeks. More than that, he hated the way she made it sound, as if he and Lainey would be finished after the party. That wasn't the case, was it?

"Tell me more about the Hungarians," he insisted. "What are they up to with The Bristols?"

"They are making moves, big moves. Laying on charm, promising to undercut our prices," Sonya said.

"What?" Yuri said. "Our prices are best wholesale, everyone knows this."

"It won't work," Dexter agreed. "The Bristols won't go for that. They made certain we understood what they were after—class and respect. We give them that."

Sonya quirked one of her perfect eyebrows at him. "You underestimate charm. It works, and the head Hungarian is good at it."

"He sent us a dead fish," Dexter reminded her.

"He is king of grand gestures."

Yuri clucked his tongue, reminding Dexter that he was *not* the king of grand gestures.

"What should we do?" Ivan asked, his glance wavering between Dexter and Sonya like they were the parents in an ugly custody dispute. If Dexter were being honest, that was how it felt some days.

"Is up to Dexter," Sonya said, giving one of those whole body shrugs the Eastern Europeans did so well. "Is what we pay him for, no? To be *sensible*."

Once again all eyes were on Dexter. "We keep doing what we're doing. If The Hungarians want to make fools of themselves, let them. Our prices, our work, and our behavior speak for us."

All the brothers looked to Sonya who took her time replying. "I agree for now. But, Dexter, barn can only keep the ponies inside for so long before they break free. Something to keep in mind." She stood and sashayed closer, bending low to whisper seductively in his ear. "You tell your little American wife hello from me, yes? I think she and I could have a lot to talk about soon." She scraped the long nail of her index finger along his shoulder and sauntered out the door.

"Are you actually happy with this guy?"

After a mostly sleepless night, Lainey had to slog through breakfast with her brother, where he threw down the gauntlet as she prepped the eggs.

Was she happy with Dexter? It shouldn't be a loaded question but it was, because of their murky future. Did the future affect the now? Should it?

"Yes."

"He doesn't seem like your type," Murphy said, regarding her with closer scrutiny than she would have liked. Normally she would have begged for the type of attention he was now bestowing on her, but not this morning. Not after she lay next to a silent Dexter for hours, pretending to sleep as he pretended to sleep, each feigning ignorance of the silent space between them.

I told you about Ian from the very beginning, she had said, unable to bear the look of hurt and betrayal on his face. It made her feel guilty, despite the fact that she didn't believe she had done anything wrong. She'd been up front, she'd told him there was someone else, even told him her humiliating part of the whole Ian ordeal. Why did he look so gutted when he already knew the truth?

It was theoretical then, was all he said, which left her wondering even more. What did that mean? Why wasn't it theoretical now? Because he knew Ian? Or because he knew her?

After that, conversation fell to zero. They lay in awkward silence, pretending to sleep for the rest of the night. At least she was pretending. Never having slept near him before, he might truly have been a silent sleeper. Like everything lately, the night hadn't gone as she thought it would and definitely not how she planned. At a minimum she wanted to nudge under his arm like a needy puppy and beg for affection. At a maximum she... Well, it was best not to go down that road. Better, probably, that the road had ended before it could be explored.

"Why isn't he my type?" Lainey asked, natural little sister defensiveness heavy in her words.

"He's so..."

Lainey scowled at Murphy, waiting for his pronouncement. What could he possibly say that was bad about Dexter? That he was boring? He wasn't, not really, not when you got to know him. Rather he was responsible and conscientious, and she liked that about him. Dexter would never be that guy who stayed up until four AM to play video games with strangers on the internet. He would never leave his child and move to Florida for the sake of alligators. He would never quit his job to make chocolate, and she liked him for that, appreciated his unyielding steadiness. Dexter was a rock. *He's* my *rock,* she thought before quickly pushing it away.

"He's so settled," Murphy said.

"What's wrong with that?" Lainey asked.

"Nothing. I like that. I'm surprised *you* like that. I've had nightmares about the kind of guy you'd end up with. It usually ended with a chest full of tattoos and a credit score in the teens. But this guy...he's solid. I think I actually approve." He held up his coffee mug toward her in a little toast.

"Me, too," she said softly, smiling, even though a big part of her heart was filled with yearning and a little bit of terror. Things had been going so well lately. Were they ruined forever? What would happen after the party?

"I always thought you had a thing for Ian," Murphy said.

"I did," Lainey confessed, sinking hard into her chair. "Ian never had a thing for me."

Murphy stared hard at her, frowning. She wasn't offended by the frown, it was his go-to expression and, inexplicably, made people love him. Lainey was overtly warm and friendly, a diehard people pleaser, and people ran from her like she had cooties; Murphy was standoffish and irascible, always did what suited him best, and people tossed themselves at his feet like he was The Pope. It was one of many lifetime contradictions she would never understand.

"I think he did," Murphy declared. "I think he always had a thing for you, too. He just wasn't ready to settle down. You know how Ian is. He's scared of the big things in life, likes to keep his options open and stay free. I think he thought…*someday*…about you. That was part of the reason I stayed here last night, to give him some time and space to think. It hit him pretty hard, finding out like this. Why didn't you warn him?"

She had no way to respond to that without telling Murphy the entire humiliating ordeal. And if she told him how she had confessed her love to Ian and almost immediately married Dexter, there would be more questions than answers. He might wonder if what was between her and Dexter was real, and should he? Was it? How did she feel, knowing Ian might actually have feelings for her?

"It's been a whirlwind," Lainey said, which was true. "Why did you think Ian had a thing for me?"

Murphy shrugged. "The way he talked about you, sort of soft. And he always wanted to see what you were up to, always asked you to tag along."

"That drove you crazy," she guessed.

He rolled his eyes. "No guy wants his little sister there to mess up his game."

"Some guys do," she said.

Murphy let out a breath and set down his coffee. "Lainey, just because I don't love you like you want me to doesn't mean I don't. Don't do this thing where you try to fit everyone into your box and then judge them because they won't."

"You do the same thing," she said, tossing her hands wide in aggravation. "You want me to be so settled, so mundane, so *blah*, to never cry, never hug you, never tell you I love you. But I'm not a robot, Murphy. I'm a little person with big emotions, and that's okay." That was the first time she had ever said those words to herself, and also the first time she felt them. And she knew exactly why she had said them and now felt them, because of Dexter. *It takes all kinds*, he had told her. Dexter was okay with her over-the-top passionate persona. Her brother should be, too.

"I know," Murphy groused. "But you wear your heart on your sleeve, kid. It worries me. I don't like to see you get hurt so much and, Lainey, you *always* get hurt." There was concern and more than a little worry in his look as he studied her.

"Dexter's a good guy," she said, the best thing she could come up with. In the beginning, a few weeks ago, she would have laughed off Murphy's concerns because of course she wouldn't be hurt. How could she be hurt by someone she didn't even care about? But now she did care, she cared a tsunami amount, and what now?

"Don't screw this up," Murphy said, pointing a finger at her. "Promise me."

"I..." she paused and took a breath, pushing through the quaver in her voice. "I'll try."

Murphy gave a nod before draining his coffee and setting it on the table with a smack. "Bring on the eggs."

"And chocolate," Lainey added cheerfully, darting to her feet to retrieve breakfast.

"And chocolate," Murphy begrudgingly added, smiling a little when she beamed.

*L*ater that day Murphy left to fly back to Florida. He had been in town for four days and she was his last stop. She tried not to be hurt by that because he was right, she couldn't make him love her the way she wanted to be loved. If she wanted to be in his life, she had to meet him where he was and accept the sort of love he was willing to give. In her imagination, she was number one, would be his first and only stop when he was in town. In Murphy's mind she was a checkmark on his long agenda of people to visit, but at least she was on the list. She would take it for what it was and not allow herself to have hurt feelings. Or maybe only a tiny amount of hurt feelings. But she did realize that Murphy didn't mean his actions to be hurtful, it was merely the way his thoughts and emotions worked, vastly different from hers, but not necessarily wrong.

She worked, throwing herself into the current project that needed to be finished. After all the dipping yesterday, that amounted to packaging and delivering her latest batch of treats. She was thankful she didn't have to have another day of chocolate mess in her kitchen, mostly because she wanted it to be clean and tidy when Dexter arrived home. Maybe the physical lack of clutter would lead to some emotional spring cleaning. At some point they needed to have a conversation. Lainey wasn't averse to talking about difficult things. The problem was that Dexter played things too close to his chest. She wanted to know where he stood before she put herself out there. What she wanted, she realized, was a grand gesture. But that wasn't Dexter's way. Should she do what she did with Murphy and accept him as he was—reserved and subdued—or should she hold out hope that he would miraculously ride in on a white horse and sweep her off her feet?

If she was honest, that was what she wanted. For once in her life she wanted someone to go the extra mile for her, to be big and dramatic and over the top in a display of grand passion. Not every day, not for the rest of her life, but once. Was that too much to ask? Was it settling to let go of that, or was it being a reasonable grownup?

She had similar questions about her job. She could admit now that she hadn't been prepared to quit her job and start a new career. She had been too hasty, too quixotic. *Like my dad.* Her savings were gone, and now what? How deep a hole should she dig while waiting on a miracle?

No one is coming to rescue you, she realized. That was disappointing, but also somewhat empowering to admit because it meant she still had hope of recovery. She was in a hole, but she wasn't buried. There was still time to dig herself out of the mess she had created. Thanks to Dexter, she wasn't in debt—yet. But she would be soon, if she didn't do something.

She closed her eyes. *I can be a grownup. I can make hard decisions, using my brain instead of my heart. I can do what's best instead of what feels good.* The little pep talk worked. When it was finished, she opened her eyes and reached for her phone, pressing the button for Mr. Weaver, the candy man.

Two hours later, she had accepted a new part time job that would bring a much needed cash infusion. She also cleaned her house and washed all her laundry. For the moment she had no projects to work on, so she picked up a book and read until she heard Dexter's car in the drive. She placed the book on the couch and sat on her hands, waiting. Lainey had a lot to tell him. Would he realize her attempts to get herself in check were an attempt to make herself a presentable prospect? *I am not a mess,* she told herself. *I'm not a damsel in need of a rescue anymore. I'm an equal partner, a healthy and whole woman. A wife.*

She bit her lip and stared at the door, heart thumping as she waited for it to open.

It didn't, though. Her phone beeped with a text. She read it with more than a little dread.

I'm zonked. Going to stay in tonight and catch up on some things/rest.

She blinked at her phone, certain she must have read it wrong. Dexter wasn't coming? Dexter was dodging her? After she'd spent the whole day reordering her life, cleaning up the dregs of her previous emotional implosions?

Okay, she replied, because what else could she say? Clearly there would be no grand gesture, and maybe that was fine. Real life didn't always work the way you planned. Sometimes, more often than not really, you had to settle for average. Lainey could do average. She was accepting an average level of care from her brother. She could do the same with Dexter. Unless he didn't even want average. Maybe this was his way of telling her he wanted nothing at all.

On the other side of their shared wall, she heard him reach for his frying pan and begin preparing his sad bachelor meal of a lone hamburger. Lainey felt confused and disheartened, but no more so than before this all began. Maybe everything would go back to the way it had been before, each of them sticking to their own apartment, everything separate and *alone*. So very alone.

Or was that the way he wanted it because she was too much? *Don't screw this up, Lainey.* Her own brother had said that to her because he knew her tendency. She would always and forever be too much. Dexter had taken longer than some to realize, but now apparently he was catching on. Lainey wasn't worth the trouble. And now she didn't have her dream job as consolation. In fact she had nothing so she grabbed her book and went upstairs. It was better to stop thinking and feeling. Maybe that was how other people survived the unending monotony of everyday life, working jobs they hated, navigating diffi-cult relationships that left them unfulfilled. Maybe they turned off their emotions and used every distraction available to blunt their pain. Lainey had tried to embrace life fully, to live in the moment and feel all the joy and pain of it. But that wasn't to be, she could see that now.

So instead of crying herself to sleep, like she normally might have, she read until her eyes drooped then turned on the television, watching reruns of one of her favorite shows until she finally drifted unaware into slumber.

CHAPTER 24

In Dexter's mind, he wasn't ignoring Lainey. When he had important decisions to make, he liked to have space and time to think clearly. Lainey, in turn, left supper for him each night on his doorstep, seemingly affirming his choice to give her some space. He assumed he was providing her the same consideration he would want, never guessing that each night he remained home felt like another rejection. If he had realized he was hurting her, he would have been appalled. As it was, he congratulated himself on exercising the discipline it took to give her what he assumed was much-needed mental clarity.

For the first time in a long time, he felt lonely and...sad? Was it sadness if you felt like your heart was somewhere outside your body? For instance, on the other side of a shared wall. He could hear Lainey moving around on her side. Occasionally he paused, coming to a complete halt as he placed his palm on the wall with what could only be called longing. He missed her. Kind of a lot. Kind of desperately. But she needed to decide what she wanted and, in Dexter's mind, the only way to do that was to have time and clearance to think.

After the party we'll talk, he told himself, which was an okay thing to tell himself because the party was coming quickly, too fast, really. The speed of its approach brought an unyielding sort of panic because what if...

But, no. If it came to that, he would figure something out. He would fix it because that was what he always did. He took care of things. He was that guy. He took care of Lainey, and he would take care of any misgivings she might have. Surely this time apart was giving her the mental clarity she needed. He simply had to hold out a while longer.

The space wasn't working well for him, though. In addition to missing her, he'd started not sleeping well, for the first time in his life. He got it now, why insomnia was such a bear. He started off fine, fading into a heavy sleep like someone who was mentally and emotionally exhausted, which he was, and then he would wake with a start, consumed by thoughts that wouldn't stop, overwhelmed by all the what-ifs currently lingering over him like a guillotine. And then, try as he might, he couldn't get back to sleep. The closer it got to the party, the worse his insomnia became. And when he woke, the only reasonable solution seemed to go to Lainey and hash everything out right then, but he wouldn't let himself. *She needs space to think; I can give her that much. I can give her anything.*

So instead he would try to read or watch television, but it never worked to distract him completely, and certainly not enough to get back to sleep.

When he woke with a gasp the night before the party, his heart sank. *Not tonight, not when I need sleep so badly to be my best.* But as he reached for the remote, he saw someone standing silently beside his bed and yelped.

"Bah! Lainey, what are you doing here?" he asked, his tone an odd combination of terror and desperation.

"I had a bad dream," she said.

His heart thumped out of control. Not from fright, he realized, but from the sight of her. He had missed her and his heart apparently hadn't been beating enough with the lack of her. Now that it had her back again, it was making up for lost time.

"What was the dream?" he asked, voice scratchy with longing. He gripped the sheet to stop his hand from reaching for her.

"I dreamed my husband was ignoring me," she said, voice breaking pathetically on the last word as she dashed at her eyes.

He sat up, perplexed. "I wasn't ignoring you. I was giving you space. I thought that was what you wanted, why you were leaving me food."

She dropped her hands to her sides and blinked at him. "I didn't want space; I hate space. I was leaving you food as a gesture, so you'd understand I wanted you to come back."

They stared at each other, each realizing they had been allowing the other what they both wanted instead of what the other needed or wanted in return. "What did you want?" he whispered.

"You," she wobbled, falling into him when he reached for her and pulled her into bed beside him in one swift motion.

"You're an actual acrobat," she whispered, hands smoothing his temples.

"I'm only getting started," he said. It would have been the perfect moment for a kiss, but he needed a minute to look at her, to study the changes that had taken place the last few days, to smell her Lainey smell, and just *be*. He adored her, his little neighbor/wife, and he had no idea how to tell her, how to keep her after their deal was over. The weight of that threatened to pull him under; he pushed it away.

"I missed you so much," she said, tears leaking out her eyes and rolling down her cheeks.

"I missed you more," he said, using his thumbs to wipe them away.

"You look different. So many cells died and I didn't get to say goodbye," she said, fingertips smoothing over his cheeks.

"You're insane," he said, but he couldn't stop smiling.

"More so now," she agreed.

"How was your visit with Murphy?" he asked. *Did you talk about Ian? Did you talk about me?* Apparently he was that guy now, the one who wanted to know if a girl was gossiping over him. That was what Lainey did to him; she made him *that guy* in every iteration he never thought he'd become.

"Good. We hashed some things out. Turns out he and I are different, dramatic gasp, and we're going to be okay with that."

"Relieved sigh," Dexter said, smiling impossibly harder when she giggled. He'd missed the giggle; he'd missed the insanity; he'd missed everything.

"How are The Russians?" Lainey asked.

"Still certifiable, but in an indiscernible language," he said.

"And Sonya?" she said. Was it his hopeful imagination that her tone sharpened on Sonya's name? Not that he wanted her to be jealous of… oh, who was he kidding? Of course he did.

"Is still Sonya," he said, thumb skimming along her jaw.

"Hmm."

There was a part of him, a big part, that wanted to ask about Ian, that wanted to dwell on his rival and Lainey's affection for him. Did she still love the man? For that matter, did she love him? He thought she did, but she was also one of those warm loving people who was warm and loving to everyone, not merely the people who were special to her. Not like Dexter, who would never cuddle with anyone else or let down his guard this way with anyone else.

"Are you ready for the party tomorrow?" he said in lieu of anything worse.

She shook her head.

"No?" he said.

"No, I mean yes, but it's after midnight. The party is today. Are you ready?"

"Yes," he said, but it came out like a question. This would be the public viewing of a marriage that had heretofore been private. Previously it had only been for pretend. Now that it was about to go public, was it real or only in his head?

"You look very serious all of a sudden," Lainey noted.

"I guess I'm a little nervous about the party," he admitted. *And everything that comes after.*

"Afraid The Russians won't behave?" she said.

"No, okay yes. I've threatened them within an inch of their lives to be on their best behavior, tried hard to impress upon them how many of our bigwig clients will be in attendance. But you never know with them. And, I have to say, The Hungarians have been hitting them hard and heavy lately."

"I saw the billboard," Lainey said. "It was kind of funny, my loyalty to The Russians notwithstanding."

"It was," Dexter agreed. He rested his head on his arm, hand still cupping her face. Lainey clutched his shirt in both her fists, snuggling closer.

"I took the job," she whispered.

"How do you feel about that?" he asked.

"Disappointed and responsible, so like a real grownup, I suppose."

"I'm sorry," he said.

"Not your fault. In fact it was only because of you I delayed the inevitable and got to live the dream a while longer. So thank you."

His face morphed into a frown. It felt wrong for her to thank him. "I should have done more."

"You did all you could. A contractual husband can only do so much."

There. She broached the subject both of them had been trying so hard to avoid. "Maybe for a little while we could forget the contractual part," he suggested, unable to believe he'd had the nerve.

Lainey smiled. "Are you propositioning me?"

He wasn't, not at all. He hadn't been referring to the current moment, but instead their entire future. But now that she took it that way, he didn't know how to undo it. And, if he were honest, that was what he wanted, not one night but all the nights. The words wouldn't form, though. How did a man ask a woman who was already his wife to remain his wife for the long haul? *You need grand gesture.* He could almost hear The Russians saying it.

"Yes," he said and kissed her because what could be grander than that?

A lot of things, as it turned out.

CHAPTER 25

In the morning Lainey and Dexter woke twined together like a broken Slinky, his legs with her legs, her arms with his arms, her hair in his eyes, mouth, and ears. It was hard to know where one ended and the other began. Not that they would have cared, except for the incessant pounding.

They didn't have the long, snuggly slow wakeup both of them had envisioned when they thought of this moment. Instead Lainey did a pushup, using Dexter's chest as the springboard and he clutched the headboard so he wouldn't topple out, bashing his head in the process.

"Burglespot," Lainey murmured, squinting.

"Whabby?" Dexter returned, rubbing his head.

"S'pounding for?"

He sat up, closing his eyes against the pain in his head. If the skull was supposedly so thick, why did it hurt so much to bash it on something? "Pounding?"

Lainey lay back down and wriggled into the blankets, a sleepy puppy who had already forgotten the pounding that Dexter could no longer ignore.

"It's coming from your half," Dexter said, putting his hand on her shoulder to shake her.

"Fix it," she mumbled and he realized he would have to because it wasn't as if he could kick his wife out of bed to answer what was clearly a deranged person incessantly pounding on her door.

He slid out of bed and threw on his pants, tossing Lainey a regretful look. His bed might not be as comfortable and welcoming as hers, but it felt so with her in it. Maybe that was the key, not the mattress or the blankets or the comforter, but the warm and soft little wife who made him never want to leave.

He jogged down the stairs, taking them two at a time. Now that he had identified the source of the pounding, he wanted to make it stop ASAP. For that reason he opened his own door, not bothering to go through Lainey's apartment to open hers.

"Yo," he said before he even saw who it was. Not that he would have known what to say in any scenario when Ian swiveled to look at him, looking deranged and unhinged.

"I need to talk to Lainey," he said.

"She's asleep," Dexter said.

"I'm not leaving until I talk to her," he said and resumed pounding on her door, now calling her name.

"Stop," Dexter said. He was used to handling men with overblown emotions, it was part of his everyday work with The Russians. This felt different somehow, and he finally realized why: his emotions were overblown, too. The sight of this man, calling Lainey's name and pounding on her door, made an unrecognizable rage begin to simmer inside him. He had his chance, and he blew it. As far as Dexter was concerned, the cards were off the table, and so was Lainey.

"Lainey," Ian called, pounding harder. "I know you're in there."

"I told you she's in there. I also told you she's asleep."

"I want to hear it from her," Ian said, now sounding desperate. "I want to hear her say that she married you, even though she loves me. Because she does, did you know? She told me so, and then a week later she married *you*. How does that make you feel? Because it makes me feel pretty bad." He swiped a hand under his nose. His hand shook, and his eyes were bloodshot, leading Dexter to believe he was hungover. Whatever he did last night had led him to this moment, meaning Dexter should cut him some slack, a hard fact to remember when all his arrows hit their marks.

But before he could fathom a reply, Lainey ducked beneath his arm and spoke. "Ian?"

Ian dropped his hand and stared at her, shell-shocked. Apparently despite the fact that he'd requested her, he couldn't quite believe he'd actually conjured her. "Lainey? You look so pretty."

She did. In fact she looked beautiful, tousle-haired and bed warm. She wore her Albert Einstein sleep shirt, and it was much more revealing than Dexter remembered, barely covering her underpants. He resisted the sudden urge to tug it down because nothing on display was Ian's to look at. And yet here he was.

"Thank you," Lainey said gently. "Ian, this is not a good time. We have our reception tonight." She glanced up at Dexter and, with a flush, quickly looked away again.

"You can't go through with that. Lainey, come *on*," Ian said. "This is me, okay?" He thumped his chest. "We've been heading somewhere for the last decade. You can't just let that go, you can't let *us* go."

"We weren't together," Lainey said.

"But you told me you love me. You *told* me. How can you just not love someone anymore?" Ian demanded.

"You didn't want me," Lainey said, which was not the rejoinder Dexter was hoping for, but he'd take it.

Ian swiped his hand over the back of his neck. "I needed time, okay? You know how my brain works. I thought...I thought we'd let it lay a bit and circle back eventually when I was ready. I had no idea it was an ultimatum, that it was then or you'd marry this..." he waved toward Dexter, apparently unable to think of an adjective bad enough to convey the depth of his loathing.

"It wasn't like that," Lainey said, now twisting her index fingers together in misery.

"Then what is it like? Because the Lainey I know wouldn't do that, wouldn't tell me she loves me and marry someone else. So what is this? What is going on? I think I deserve to know."

Lainey squeezed her eyes closed and pressed her fingers to her temples. "Ian, I'm sorry. I really am. I didn't want to hurt you, don't want to hurt you, but I cannot have this conversation right now, not today. Dexter and I have our reception tonight and it's a big deal."

"I don't care," Ian yelled.

Lainey opened her eyes. "I do. And Dexter does. And I'm not going to mess it up for him, I owe him that."

Dexter flinched. What did that mean? Was she still thinking of their contract? Would she follow through, down to the last detail, and let him go? What about last night? Was it only because he was there and Ian wasn't? He swallowed hard, feeling sick, feeling *used*. Would he have to do the walk of shame to his office?

Lainey took a steadying breath. "Please go, please. We'll grab a coffee and talk when cooler heads can prevail, all right? Are you okay to drive?"

Ian nodded, looking wobblier than his assurance credited, and turned toward his truck. Dexter and Lainey watched him go in silence. When he was fully out of sight, she turned and faced Dexter, leaning on the doorframe behind her.

"That was an eventful way to wake up. Sorry. Would you like some breakfast before you go to work? I can make eggs."

Eggs? What was she talking about? He didn't want eggs; he wanted answers. He wanted declarations. He stared down at her, trying to fathom a reply. Long practice meant his face revealed none of his thoughts or emotions, and he worked hard to keep his tone even, too, when he answered.

"No, thank you. I'm going to get an early start. Lots to do today, The Russians are leaving early to set up the party."

"Oh." Maybe he wasn't as good as he thought at keeping his pesky emotions under wraps because she was doing the blinky thing she did when her feelings were hurt.

Get in line, he thought. His feelings were hurt, too. He'd had the best night of his life, with the woman who happened to be his wife, and yet he couldn't enjoy it with the unanswered question between them. Who did Lainey love? Which one did she want to be with for the long haul?

"I should go," he said, his stupid hand reaching out so it could touch her hair. He wound a piece around his finger, staring at it.

"Okay," she said, voice soft, big eyes still watching him. "I…I have some deliveries to make this afternoon. Maybe it would be easier if I met you at the party."

There was a question in there, but he didn't know what it was. And he certainly didn't know how to answer. He felt like he was supposed to say no, that he would pick her up and they would drive together, but it didn't seem like the sensible thing when she had things to do.

"All right," he agreed.

She looked disappointed, but why? He was out of his element, over his head. All the usual tactics—being calm and reasonable—were failing him. What was left?

He had the sudden vision of himself bestowing the Kiss To End All Kisses, grabbing her, pressing her against the doorframe, then carrying her back upstairs. But of course he didn't do that. Could he even carry her all the way upstairs? Doubtful. And it felt wrong to kiss her with Ian's breakdown still hovering between them. Still, though, he stared at her lips as he waited for her to speak, wanting, yearning. There was a word he never thought he'd use to describe himself. Before he met Lainey he would have said it only applied to proper Victorian maidens. But it was the only word that could describe this persistent and unending ache inside him. He yearned for Lainey to fill the Lainey-shaped hole she'd created in his heart.

"So I'll see you tonight," the pretty lips said. "At the party." She tapped his shoulder and then she was gone, disappearing from view as she went to her side of the house and shut the door.

"See you," Dexter said, hand held aloft in a suspended wave. He formed it into a fist and stared at it, debating the merits of beating himself to a pulp for his newfound helpless stupidity.

CHAPTER 26

"Is Mr. Floppy Jowls again," Yuri proclaimed as soon as Dexter entered the office.

"Is like basset hound staring at steak, yes?" Maxim said, high fiving his brother.

Andrei tipped his head, studying Dexter. "No, is also something different. Spring in step, mixed with droopy sadness."

"Is woman trouble," Ivan added.

Yuri held up his hands. "No woman trouble on day of big party. Lots of clients coming. Must be happiness all around."

"We will be happy, *are* happy," Dexter amended.

"This is not face of happiness," Maxim said, lifting Dexter's lips and forcing them into a smile.

"Tell Popovs the trouble so we can fix before big party," Andrei commanded.

"There's no trouble. We had a rough wakeup. Some guy from Lainey's past…" he trailed off. Was Ian from her past? Or was he the future, making Dexter the placeholder? That was what he had been at first, he knew. Lainey had come to him in all honesty, broken and hurt, wanting nothing more from him than a few thousand dollars. It wasn't her fault he'd fallen in love with her. She wasn't obligated to maintain their marriage after their contract expired. But he wanted her to. More than anything, and the feeling was so out of control it left him helpless enough to consult the Popovs.

"Is like hearing thirteen year old girl read diary out loud," Yuri said, pressing his hands over his ears. "Dexter, take advice. Be man. Time for grand gesture."

"I don't even know what that means," Dexter admitted. He realized how far he'd fallen when Yuri's eyes lit with excitement.

"Two words: white horse and knight costume. Good thing for you I know man who rents both. Also broadsword, if things go bad."

When he slit a finger across his throat, a bit of sense returned to Dexter's brain. He held up his hand, warding off the crazy. "Thanks, guys, but this is something I need to figure out on my own. Let me know if there's anything you need me to handle for the party."

"Is under control," Ivan assured him.

"You figure out wife problem," Andrei said.

"Happy faces," Maxim reminded him, pulling his own lips into a grimace that was probably supposed to pass for a happy visage and instead looked like a plague death mask.

Dexter nodded and backstepped away from them, locking himself in his office. He let out the breath he didn't know he'd been holding and tried to think. For so long he had been trying to love Lainey the way he thought she wanted to be loved—with lots of space and time and low-key interactions. But that wasn't Lainey's style. *You need a grand gesture.*

As much as he hated to admit it, he thought The Russians were probably right, at least in this instance. Lainey was a grand gesture kind of girl. For her, he could do it; he could do anything. The question was what should he do?

He sat behind his desk and stared blankly at his computer until at last inspiration struck. Then he reached for his phone. This would be the grandest gesture of his life. If it didn't work, he would likely never recover. Either way, Lainey was worth it.

*L*ainey was nervous. Unable to eat, have-to-stop-thinking-about-it levels of nervous. During the day she kept properly busy, working a few hours in the morning for Mr. Weaver, then making deliveries of her own candy in the afternoon. So far her new boss didn't have a problem with her side business, and she thought it was due more to patheticness on her part than kindness on his. Why should he be bothered by her tiny little hobby? It was no threat to his vast candy empire. Okay, maybe vast candy empire was a stretch, but he did have the Easter and Valentine markets clearly cornered. Lainey would never be proper competition. Why shouldn't she piddle with her adorable little hobby? That was what she imagined him thinking. In reality he was probably too distracted by his painful lumbago to care what she was doing, one way or the other. Having her on staff had drastically reduced the number of hours he had to stand, and for that he was almost gleeful.

When she was finished making her deliveries, it was time to get ready for the party. From her former working days, she owned a proper black evening gown. Last week she tried it on, to make certain she hadn't grown out of it over the months of sampling her wares. Thankfully poverty and hard work made her balance all the sampling with not eating anything else, so it was a sad kind of win. She hadn't gained weight, but she had probably shaved years off her life with malnutrition. If not for the milk in the chocolate and all the orange peel she'd used in the chocolate covered fruitcakes at Christmas, she would definitely have rickets and scurvy by now.

That could be my thing; I could bring back all the obscure pirate diseases. Maybe I'll get a parrot, add a bird disease to the mix.

Tonight she did not look like a pirate, thankfully. There was no way she could compete with the exquisite Sonya, but who could? If one were to take Sonya out of the equation, however, Lainey could hold her own. She had curled her hair, the first time since she quit her job, and applied full makeup. Her mascara had become so gunky she had to look up a life hack to figure out how to fix it and she was certain there was more than a little bacteria on all the implements that had sat fallow for so many months, but hopefully the conjunctivitis would hold off until tomorrow, allowing her to get through this most momentous night before the temporary blindness set in. *There's always a bright side, if you look hard enough with your conjunctivitis-swollen lids,* Lainey thought. And if she had to get an eye patch, more the better for her retro pirate identity.

Why was the night momentous? She had no idea. None of these people meant anything to her. The only ones she knew were The Russians. But for Dexter and his career, the night was momentous. For that reason, it was important to her. There was more to it, however, and that was the part she had been trying not to dwell on. The night had taken on its own significance, outside of Dexter's job. Increasingly it began to feel like a do or die event, a make it or break it test run on their marriage. Mostly because they had set it up that way. Why hadn't they talked about what would happen after? In all the time they'd spent together the last few weeks, why had they never addressed the issue of their future?

Was it because, like her, Dexter was afraid? Or, worse, was it because he didn't care? Would he be glad to be rid of her and her problems? When she thought about it, she had been nothing but a drain on him, both financially and otherwise. His stoic nature must be so tired of her leaky eyes and emotions. The one thing he had asked was that she didn't make him try to fix her, and what had he done? Fixed her in every possible way. For a while it had been like having her own tagalong life coach, teaching her how to be a better and more productive human. Even if it all fell apart, she would be forever grateful for everything he'd taught her, like how to take responsibility for her life, how to switch off her over eager emotions and embrace duty, how to appreciate herself, even if most people thought she was needy and off kilter. On the other hand, what was the true cost of all those lessons? It would be ironic indeed if, in teaching her how to handle herself in the real world, Dexter had exhausted his patience and needed to walk away. On the other hand, she would understand. Hadn't she always believed she was too much? His absence would be definitive proof, once and for all. It would be a devastating blow if the one person who finally made her see her worth robbed her of it in the process of leaving.

Right now, however, she only had to focus on the moment at hand. She might not have her life together, might still fail at everything, but for this night she looked amazing. Better, she looked like a loving and happy wife.

Am I? she asked, studying herself in the mirror. One eye winked closed. She hoped it was because she was thinking about the possibility of pinkeye and not an actual case of pinkeye. Forcing both eyes open, she blinked a couple of times and gave herself another pep talk.

For tonight, you're the happiest, luckiest woman in the world. When tomorrow comes...we'll deal with it then.

She opened her fancy clutch, plopped her lipstick inside and turned to go, pausing in the kitchen to dump a handful of chocolates inside. If Lainey's life had taught her one thing, it was that one never knew when there might be an emergency when chocolate was required. And as far as Lainey was concerned, every emergency required chocolate.

She snapped the clutch closed, gave it a little pat, and walked out the door, ready to meet her husband.

The Russians were full of contradictions. Dexter learned the lesson early. To most people, they didn't follow discernable patterns. Dexter's mother was Polish, however, giving him some insight into how the minds of Eastern Europeans worked. For instance three years ago the brothers spent four days on the phone trying to hash out which office toilet paper was the cheapest, finally locating a half ply made from recycled trash in Taiwan. For three months that was their standard until Yuri got an unmentionable infection from it that required a ten-day course of antibiotics. But those same men who had happily skimped on toilet paper that cost ten cents less per role had rented out an entire luxury country club for Dexter's reception, complete with full catering by some of the biggest names in the food industry.

True, everything was a tax write-off because it was essentially a networking party. Also true that the catering was a goodwill PR stunt to fluff up some of their clients. But still, it had cost a fortune and been a massive amount of work. Dexter knew because he'd watched the brothers oversee every step of the process. He was touched by their thoughtfulness and care. Even if it had started out as a stunt to cover their backsides after their slipup at The Bristol, it had turned into so much more. In their way, they were telling Dexter they loved and appreciated him, and maybe that they were a little bit sorry for all the sleepless nights they'd brought him the last few years of putting out fires and rescuing them from themselves. They would not be where they were as a company without him, Dexter knew. He had brought them from a humble warehouse on the docks to a fancy office in a prime location, to say nothing of the explosive growth of their client list and portfolio. But he owed them something, too. In their own way, they had given him something in return; they had taught him not to take life or himself too seriously, to find the value in people who were so unlike himself. If he got down to the nitty-gritty, they had helped prepare him for Lainey, helped him to see beyond her zany exterior to the adorably sweet woman within. He could never repay them for that, not with all the money or prestigious clients in the world.

All he could do was play his part tonight. The Bristols, and everyone else, would see nothing but a happy groom and an upstanding family company with a rock solid work ethic. This was technically Dexter and Lainey's night, but The Popovs would shine bright; Dexter would make sure of it.

There was a rustle, the sort that happens when a beautiful woman enters the room, as if everyone has to stop and stare, arrested by the sight. Dexter turned, expecting to see Lainey, but saw Sonya instead, her cool beauty fully on display in a midnight blue dress that matched her eyes and conformed to her lush figure. Dexter easily and readily admitted she was beautiful, but in an abstract way. It wasn't the sort of beauty that touched him, not the way Lainey's beauty pierced his heart, almost painful in its overwhelming depth and size.

As if thinking about her had conjured her, he noticed her slip in quietly behind Sonya, with no fuss or undue attention, which was a shame because he thought she looked stunning. He loved her in her ubiquitous messy bun, adored her in an apron covered with chocolate, and now had a newfound devotion to the Albert Einstein nightshirt. But this was a whole other level and he couldn't look away.

"Dexter," Sonya said, her tone perplexed.

Dexter paused, tearing his eyes off Lainey with effort in order to regard Sonya. "What?"

She shook her head at him and he realized what happened. When he began walking toward the entrance, she thought he was coming to her heel, as every man in the room minus her brothers seemingly longed to do. But in his haste to reach Lainey, he had completely forgotten Sonya until she spoke.

"Thanks for coming," he said lamely and kept going until he reached his goal, until he reached Lainey. Then he did what he had been longing to do the entire day—he pulled her close and kissed her, wrapping her in what had to be the world's tightest hug. "I missed you," he said, an understatement. The day had felt interminable.

"Same," she said, returning his hard squeeze. "How was your day?"

"Long, but better now. Yours?"

"Same."

"You look incredible," he said, kissing the top of her head. "What are the chances we could leave right now without being noticed?"

"Since you're the guest of honor, I'm going to say not great," she said, easing back slightly to touch his tie. She stood on her toes to whisper in his ear. "But maybe we could find a private moment, before The Russians find us."

"Lainey, you are here," Ivan boomed.

Too late, Dexter mouthed.

"You can tell Lainey is here because Dexter is no longer Mr. Floppy Jowls," Maxim added.

Lainey's brows rose questioningly toward Dexter who wound his finger around his ear.

"Is time to make introductions, yes?" Yuri added.

"Yes," Dexter agreed with a nod. He would be the one to introduce Lainey, both because she was his wife and because he was the official Popov spokesperson. "Ready?" He stared down at Lainey, trying not to beam. Perhaps he actually was Mr. Floppy Jowls without her because, now that he thought about it, he was almost always smiling when they were together. It was probably a nice break for his face when he was away and not grinning like a deranged person.

"Put me in, coach," Lainey said, slipping her hand in his and giving it a squeeze.

Unable to resist, he leaned down to whisper in her ear. "I think you're my favorite."

"Your favorite wife?" she guessed.

"My favorite everything," he said. He squeezed her hand, noting with pleasure the resulting flush that crept over her cheeks. Suddenly it felt like everything would be okay. Lainey was here. The night was perfect. What could possibly go wrong?

Everything, as it turned out.

For a while, everything was fine. Dexter had always been good with names and faces, a bonus when he was the de facto spokesman of his company. He introduced Lainey to each person they encountered, remembering to tell her a pertinent fact he hoped was interesting.

Lainey responded like a seasoned pro, so well that if he ever decided to run for office, she'd be a shoe-in as a senatorial wife. She smiled, she dazzled, she charmed, responding with sincere wit and warmth, nothing fake or awkward about her.

The Russians trooped silently behind them, looking stern and broody. They weren't, and Dexter thought Lainey's bubbly enthusiasm went a long way toward providing a proper contrast. The brothers must have thought so too because they began to relax as the night wore on, occasionally laughing or smiling at something she said.

By the time they sat down to eat, it was as if she had become an honorary Popov, especially when she spent so long extolling each bite of her meal.

"Is this beef from heaven? I don't know what a tournedo is, but it is about a thousand times better than a tornado," she said.

"To be fair, you've never eaten a tornado," Dexter said.

"There's a lot you don't know about me," she said, resting her hand on his thigh so he lost the thread of the conversation a few minutes.

When he came back to earth, he realized she was cutting her meat in ever-tinier bites.

"What are you doing?" he asked.

"If you cut it in tiny bites, it makes more," she said.

"It absolutely does not," Dexter said.

"Of course it does," Yuri said, coming to Lainey's defense. "Is science."

"You're not a science guy," Lainey said. "It's okay."

"We each have six ounces," Dexter said, showing her his beef for comparison. "No matter how many bites you cut, it's still the same six ounces."

"No, you have six bites. Lainey has twenty. Is more," Ivan said with authority.

"More bites does not equal more," Dexter said.

"How is twenty not more than six?" Maxim asked.

"Because it was the same amount to start with," Dexter said.

"Dexter is bad at maths, too. Are we sure he should be in charge of books?" Andrei asked.

"I love you guys," Lainey said happily. The brothers beamed at her, a real smile and not the scary scowl they reserved for strangers.

"I can't handle all five of you," Dexter muttered.

"Let's also hope your tactics for us aren't the same," Lainey said, tossing him a wink as she shoveled a bite of potatoes.

"Dexter is blushing," Yuri said, pointing an oversized finger at Dexter's cheeks.

"Dexter is not blushing," Dexter said. Dexter was *flushing*. There was a difference. As surreptitiously as possible, he checked his watch. Exactly how much longer until he could have Lainey all to himself again?

"Is dance time now," Maxim declared. He signaled to someone and music began.

Lainey gasped. "Dancing? I love dancing."

"We somehow thought you might," Yuri said.

"Are you sure you are not Russian, Lainey?" Ivan asked. "You love all the good things in life—food, music, poetry. You have the passion.

Not like Dexter. Is wooden cutout Pinocchio boy." His hand encompassed Dexter with a little wave of disgust, miming a marionette.

"Yes, but where would we be without him?" Lainey asked. "We need Dexters in the world, mine specifically." She rested her hand on his thigh again, giving it a squeeze and once again Dexter's mind flew somewhere near the ceiling and hovered, the very best sort of out-of-body experience.

"Ask your wife to dance," Andrei commanded, slugging Dexter's shoulder with what was probably supposed to be a gentle tap but instead touched bone.

"I was going to," Dexter said.

"Better hurry or we will," Maxim threatened, wagging his brows.

"First dance to the husband," Ivan said, scowling at his brother. "After that, we talk."

"All the dances for the husband," Dexter said. He stood and held out his hand to Lainey.

"Dexter, be fair," Yuri complained.

"Get your own wives, don't poach mine," Dexter said.

"They're fun," Lainey said, trailing behind him as he led her away.

"They're something," Dexter agreed, tugging her tightly into his embrace as they started to sway. "I'm not a great dancer."

"I don't care," Lainey replied.

That was likely true, and also one of the things he loved about her. Lainey cared about the fundamentals and none of the trappings. "Are you having a good night?"

"The best," Lainey gushed. "It feels real."

He rested his forearm on her shoulder, cupping her face. "Isn't it?"

She bit her lip and gazed up at him with what was either a pensive or hopeful expression. He felt like he was holding his breath as he awaited her answer.

"I…" she began, but was soon interrupted.

"Is good time to cut in, yes?"

They swiveled in unison to see Sonya on standby, perfectly posed and perfectly polished. Her smile was seductive and confident.

"No, go away," Lainey said.

Sonya's exquisite features arranged themselves into an angry pout. "Is bad manners to refuse hostess a dance."

"It's worse manners to sexually harass your employee," Lainey said. She stopped dancing and faced Sonya fully.

"Lainey," Dexter said softly, warningly. He was heartened by her defense, but people were starting to look at them.

"I never," Sonya hissed.

"You always," Lainey hissed in return. "But no more. Don't touch him again. Or else."

"I need to hear it from Dexter," Sonya said, facing him.

"You have heard it from me, a thousand times," he said.

"Is game we play," she said, waving him away.

"It is not a game when you stalk another woman's husband," Lainey inserted.

Sonya returned her furious scowl to her. "Is not real marriage. Everyone knows this."

Lainey's hands settled on her hips. She took a small step forward. "Who are you to say what's real and what isn't? This is our marriage, not yours. Leave Dexter alone. I mean it."

"Big words from small American nuisance," Sonya said.

"Ladies," Dexter said, tugging nervously at his collar.

The brothers appeared on the scene, as they always did when their sister showed up. Dexter was never certain if it was an attempt to contain her or curiosity over what might happen next. This time it was neither.

"They are here," Yuri hissed, furious tone matching Sonya's.

"Who?" Dexter asked. He had a sudden sympathy for the spotter standing at the edge of *The Titanic*. The night was spinning away from him with alarming speed.

"The Hungarians," Ivan said. As a unit, all of them turned to the entrance where, indeed, The Hungarians had just entered.

They were a good counterpart to The Russians, all of them sandy haired and fair skinned, as opposed the The Russians' black hair, brows, and expressions. While The Russians looked like someone you might encounter in a back alley if you forgot to pay hush money, The

Hungarians were more dapper, at home among the elite of the foodie world.

"How dare they," Andrei said.

"Time to kill them, yes?" Maxim said.

"Let's all take a deep breath and regroup," Dexter suggested, but he was certain no one heard. And when a new voice arrived on the scene, he had to take his own breath.

"Lainey, we need to talk," Ian said. While everyone was focused on The Hungarians, he had arrived through the opposite door unseen.

"It's our reception," Dexter said. "I've been patient, but you can't be here. You have to go."

"Not until I hear it from Lainey," Ian said, sounding no less desperate than he had that morning at their house.

Everyone turned to Lainey, waiting for her answer, but before she could provide it someone else spoke.

"Popovs. Nice little shindig you have here," Blaise Kovacs interrupted. He was the oldest Hungarian brother, their de facto leader. Tonight he wore a tuxedo, one that looked like it had been made for him.

"You look like ventriloquist dummy that lost its hand," Yuri said, scowling. "Go back to Edgar Bergen, Charlie McCarthy. Is waiting for dummy to start show."

Blaise gave an unpleasant little laugh and scanned Yuri up and down. "You look like a grizzly wearing pants."

"All the better to eat you with," Ivan said, popping his knuckles.

"Lainey," Ian pressed.

Lainey crossed her arms over her chest, looking distressed.

Dexter would have to make a scene, but so be it. The time for polite discourse was over, and Ian needed to go. But before he could say so, Sonya spoke up.

"Why don't you go off with your little American friend and talk? Leave Dexter to us." Her hand reached out, curling possessively on Dexter's bicep.

Lainey straightened, uncrossed her arms, and forced them to her sides. "I told you not to touch him. Ever again," she said carefully, and then she pounced.

For a breathless few seconds the men stood in a circle, watching the women have what could only be a catfight in the center of the ballroom. They scrambled back and forth, rolling together like warring anacondas as they pulled each other's hair, shoved, bit, and scratched. It was as mesmerizing as it was disturbing and everyone seemed unable to look away.

Ian was the first to react. "Lainey!" He reached both arms, apparently intent on pulling her back, and that was too much for Dexter.

"She's not yours to rescue," he said, and now Ian turned to him, taking a swing. Dexter was prepared for it. He rebounded and took a swing of his own, one Ian returned.

The Hungarians and The Russians surveyed each other. Then, with a shrug, pounced, creating an instant melee of Eastern European grunts as fists met flesh.

With a high keening sound, Mrs. Popov jumped into the fray, fake leather knockoff *Kate Spadd* pocketbook upraised, beating anyone she could find, which unfortunately happened to be one of her sons, more often than not.

No one could tell who was winning, or if anyone was. At one point everyone was in a twelve person tangle together, struggling and wrestling for supremacy, until at last the police finally arrived, cuffed everyone, and led them away.

CHAPTER 28

"So that's it," Lainey said. They finally let her access her purse. She'd created a little tasting tray for the officers, who finally relented about halfway through her tale, devouring the chocolates one by one in the proper order. "I married a stranger for money, at least at first. And you can see why Sonya had to be stopped."

"You're right, the strawberry does taste better after the lemon," one of the officers, Adam, said.

"I think what we have here, Lainey, is a failure to communicate," Officer Taylor added, licking a dollop of melted chocolate off his thumb.

"How so?" Lainey asked.

"We heard your version, we heard Dexter's version, we heard unintelligible rumblings from The Russians, The Hungarians tried to offer us a bribe, and Sonya hit on us."

"Everything sounds in order," Lainey said.

"What's missing is some direct communication between you and your husband," Adam said.

"Are you a marriage counselor?" Lainey asked.

"By now he could be. Guy's on his third marriage," Taylor said.

"Tell me I'm wrong," Adam challenged.

"You're not wrong," Taylor agreed. His chair scraped hard on the cement as he pushed away from the table and stood. "On that note, sit tight a little longer, Mrs. Niemen. You're still our prisoner."

"You got any more candy?" Adam asked, pausing by the door.

"At home. I'll drop some off tomorrow," Lainey promised.

He tapped the door and exited. A minute later the door opened and Dexter was pushed through, rubbing his wrists. Lainey wondered what the officers told him because he seemed surprised to see her sitting there.

"Lainey. Are you okay?"

"I don't know. Look into my eyes. Can you feel the crazy spreading?" Lainey asked.

He winced. "Okay, I probably shouldn't have said that. I was a little panicked when they first brought us in. I've never been arrested before." He edged closer until he stood directly in front of her. She stood, nervously clasping her hands behind her back.

"You weren't wrong, Dexter. I am kind of crazy. I'm a lot of work, too much. Everything went wrong, and it was all my fault. And I made you break the contract because you tried so hard to fix me. Too hard, especially because I'm unfixable, and..."

He shook his head and rested his hands on her shoulders, looking deep into her eyes to stop her torrent of self-flagellation. "Don't say that. There was nothing to fix, nothing at all. You are perfect and wonderful and amazing, exactly as you are." He picked her up, bringing her eye level. "You once asked me what *married* meant, and I didn't have an answer because we weren't married, because I didn't understand. But now I do. Being married means being all in, doing the hard work it takes to be with that person, even when you don't feel like it, over and over again, day after day, but in some miraculous way it's not a drudge. It becomes the best part of you, the best part of everything. All I wanted from this arrangement was to fix my wonky job situation. In exchange I got so much more. I got everything because I got you. I love you, Lainey. I love you so much. I adore everything about you. On paper we're total opposites, and in the real world, too. But I don't care because I love everything that makes us different. It makes no rational sense, the way I feel for you, and I've never been happier to be so irrational. I know there's Ian standing between us, but I think if you give me a chance, I can be a good husband. I can be that guy who adores you, for the rest of our lives."

"About that, about Ian. Here's what I figured out, thanks to you. Dexter, when I was a kid, no one noticed me. No one cared for me in the way I wanted to be cared for. My dad's world centered around his dreams. My mom, when she was alive, centered around my dad. Murphy was independent and didn't need anyone. And there I was, in my own Lainey orbit, desperately wanting to be loved. When Ian came along, it seemed like the answer to a prayer. He paid attention to me. He was *kind* to me. He let me tag along with him and Murphy. When I was with him, it seemed like enough because he gave me more than anyone else ever had. But it was never enough, not really. It was better than what I had before, but it wasn't complete. I told myself that gaping hole that remained was because he and I weren't together, and if we were ever together, it would be fixed.

"But then you came along, and I understood everything that had been missing. Ian doesn't want me, not really. When his possessive jealousy dies down, he'll realize and understand that. He had ten years and he never made a move until I took myself out of reach. And the truth, the wonderful and amazing truth, is that I don't want Ian, not anymore. He and I would never have worked because we're too alike. We're both dreamers, romantics, passionate nomads looking for our tent stakes. You, you're a tent stake, *my* tent stake. You don't talk about love, you *love*. You cover me when I'm cold, wipe my face when it's covered in strawberries, wash my dishes, hold me when I'm asleep, defend my packages from the box people. You are everything I need and everything I didn't know I wanted. You're it, you're the total package, you're my Mr. Darcy and Mr. Rochester rolled into one. I dream of you every minute I'm awake, and all of them when I'm asleep. And oh my goodness, Dexter, I love you so, so, *so* much." She was predictably crying by the end of her speech. Dexter was torn between wanting to kiss her and wanting to dry her tears. In the end he did both, kissing her lips while using his thumbs to dry her cheeks.

"I have to sit, because as much as I want to be the guy who can hold you endlessly, I'm not." He sank into the chair, Lainey in his lap.

"That was very courageous, to tell me you loved me when you thought I still loved Ian," Lainey said. She kissed his cheek, pausing to inhale.

"The Russians told me I needed a grand gesture."

"So wise, The Russians," Lainey said, smiling when he rolled his eyes. "In this instance, at least."

"In this instance," he agreed. "Although telling you I loved you wasn't the gesture; that was common sense after our ordeal."

Lainey perked up, wriggling a little. "There's more?"

"There's more, so much more." His hand rubbed a preemptively soothing circle on her back because what he was about to tell her was momentous. "I quit my job."

She blinked at him, frozen with shock. "Come again now."

"I'm a nine-to-five guy, Lainey. I'm happy to go to work and come home, it's all I need. But you, you have dreams, and I love that about you. I don't want you to give up your dream."

"But I failed at my dream," Lainey reminded him.

"You didn't fail. Look how much you learned. All you need is another boost," he said.

She thought he was being generous about that but didn't quibble. "How is you quitting your job going to give me a boost?"

"Well, this is the grand part. Don't be mad." He tried to gauge her reaction, but he couldn't because she had no idea what he was about to say. "I bought the candy store."

She couldn't be certain what he said because her heart jumped into her ears, obscuring all sound. "What? Did you say you bought the candy store? Mr. Weaver's candy store? The candy store where I work? My favorite candy store? My comfort place since I was a little girl?"

"Yes. Mr. Weaver has agreed to stay on and show us the ropes for a while as we make the transfer, to mentor us so we make sure and get it right. I'll do all the boring backroom stuff that I normally do, and you'll be the front room person, the creative force, the maker of garish candy ants and so much more." He touched the hair at her temple, smoothing it affectionately with a fond smile.

Her mouth opened and a little puff of air escaped, her last. It was a while before she remembered to breathe again and then she sucked hard, trying to take in enough oxygen to make her brain function again. Words, she needed to say words. Instead she burst into tears.

"You're not happy?" he guessed, feeling no small amount of his own panic.

She shook her head.

"You are happy?" he tried.

She shook her head.

"I'm going to need some form of understandable communication here soon. If you don't want the store, we can undo it. I haven't signed anything yet; we have a gentleman's agreement."

She clutched his lapels. "I can't believe you out-dreamed me."

"What?"

"The dream, my dream, it wasn't big enough. Not with you, not with the job. Everything is so much more than I even knew I wanted, and I...Are we really going to get to work together every day?"

"That's the best dream of all, huh?" he guessed, petting her hair again. He had loved working with her in the evenings, and he thought she felt the same.

She nodded, swiping at her ruined mascara. "The best, the very best."

The door opened and Officer Adam poked his head inside. "Everything okay in here? We're watching through the mirror, obviously, but we can't read lips and Lainey's crying."

Lainey nodded. "It's Robert. He's spectacular."

Adam squinted, confused. "Who's Robert?"

Lainey pointed to Dexter.

"It's Dexter," Adam said.

"Where?" Lainey and Dexter said together.

"Medusa eyes of crazy," Adam muttered as he put up his hands and backed slowly out of the room.

Lainey rested her head on Dexter's shoulder. "Not that I'm not ecstatic for us, because I am, but what about The Russians? I don't want to leave them in the lurch."

"I found a replacement for me," Dexter said.

"Who?" Lainey asked.

"Sonya. She's the only other person the brothers listen to and she has a pretty good head for business, after you dig through a few terrifying layers. Plus as my wise wife once said, 'sometimes you have to fight crazy with crazy.' Sonya will either out-crazy or out-charm anyone she encounters. It's time to stop fighting the crazy and let The Russians learn to make it work for them."

"Are you sure she can handle it?" Lainey asked.

The door opened again. This time Officer Taylor poked his head in. "You lovebirds are free to go."

"We're not being charged?" Dexter said.

"We, uh, had a conversation with Sonya. She made us see that charges weren't necessary for anyone but The Hungarians who were clearly trespassing."

"Yeah, I think she's going to be okay," Lainey said. She stood and held out her hand to Dexter. "Let's go home and move your stuff into my side of the house. No offense, but your lack of clutter creeps me out."

"It will be good to save on rent, now that we have no income," he said. "After we're done moving my stuff, we can talk about a budget."

She kissed his palm and tossed him a promising little look. "You think so?"

"Or maybe some other time," he amended, clearing his throat. "In any case, let's go home, sweetest wife." He slipped his arm around her shoulders.

She slid her arm around his waist and gave him a squeeze in return. "Let's go home, best husband."

Behind them The Russians eased out of the various rooms where they'd been held, following silently behind Lainey and Dexter as if they were pied pipers.

Sonya was waiting for them in the parking lot, arms crossed impatiently as she leaned on her car. She rounded up her brothers, signaling them to get into the waiting car with a nod of her head. They did so, tossing Lainey a combined and surreptitious wave.

Lainey and Sonya eyed each other and shared a nod.

"What was that about?" Dexter asked, opening the passenger door of his car for Lainey.

"Sonya and I have reached an understanding. She won't poach my territory anymore."

"I'm your territory?" he said, leaning over the console to press his face to her neck and inhale her wonderful and perfect Lainey smell. *Chocolate. Vanilla. Love. Home.*

"Yes, but we should go home so I can make certain you're properly marked," Lainey said, closing her eyes as his lips pressed her pulse point. "How fast can you drive?"

"As fast as the law allows," Dexter replied, easing away to start the car.

"Ten miles over?" she prodded. Her hand reached out and settled on his thigh, giving it a little squeeze.

"Five," he agreed. But then she smiled her Lainey smile, and he was gone.

In the end he drove twenty miles over the speed limit, and he didn't fuss when he got pulled over. Especially not when the officer's radio crackled and Officer Adam's voice filtered out.

"Let the lovebirds go. They've got places to be."

With a roll of his eyes, the officer waved them on, almost immediately distracted by the car behind them. Four men were inside, oversized, dark, and brooding, the kind of men that were always up to no good. He headed toward his car, ready to make a stop, when he was once again distracted by the driver, the most beautiful woman he'd ever seen in real life.

She paused the car, rolled down the window, and blew him a kiss. He remained riveted, stunned into place until the car passed and the spell finally broke.

With a shake of his head, he returned to his vehicle. *Weird day,* he thought. With a sudden craving for chocolate, he rooted in the small bag of personal items he kept on his floor, glancing around to make certain no one was watching. When it was clear he was fully alone, he removed the chocolate ant with the overly made up face and took a giant bite. His wife had discovered the things and bought one for him as a joke, but he was now addicted. He closed his eyes and let the chocolate work its magic, wondering what sort of person made chocolate ants for a living.

No one you'll ever meet, he assured himself. That sort of crazy would surely make itself known, warding him away. In the meantime, there was chocolate.

He took another bite, until only the ant's garish makeup face was left, then he popped it in his mouth and closed his eyes, resting his head on the seat for a moment of peace before the craziness of his night resumed.

Thank you for reading *The WINO Next Door*. For more books, please check out my website at www.vanessagraybartal.com